Fear Fortune, Father

S. B. HOUGH

FEAR FORTUNE, FATHER

S. B. HOUGH

❦ PERENNIAL LIBRARY
Harper & Row, Publishers
New York, Cambridge, Philadelphia, San Francisco
London, Mexico City, São Paulo, Sydney

A hardcover edition of this book was published in England in 1974 by Victor Gollancz Ltd. It is here reprinted by arrangement with Brandt & Brandt, Inc.

First PERENNIAL LIBRARY edition published 1984.

Library of Congress Cataloging in Publication Data

Hough, S. B. (Stanley Bennett), 1917-
    Fear fortune, father.

    Originally published: London : Gollancz, 1974.
    I. Title.
PR6058.O83F4 1984   823'.914   83-48353
ISBN 0-06-080679-6 (pbk.)

84 85 86 87 88 10 9 8 7 6 5 4 3 2 1

"You can't do it and not tell them," she said. "It would be just the same as stealing."

"Why not?" I said. I put on my philosophic and didactic expression and looked straight at her. "All other moral values are being questioned these days, so why should we not question that one?"

She looked nonplussed. She liked to be modern.

I

I WAS WALKING down the crowded High Street in Lockley when it started to rain. It was October and we were having showers. I sheltered in a doorway. I had got over the feeling about not being able to go into a pub or a café to shelter; or I thought that I had.

I had seen myself getting into the passive state in which I had to accept things. I did not like it. I was wearing my better suit and coat, and they were going to get wet. I suppose that was the point. It came either too soon or too late, and I found I had not that much acceptance.

Even I knew it was false, to be in a frame of mind in which I did not wish to be seen sheltering in doorways. The people going past and looking out of car windows were not going to notice and start saying, "Look, there's old Pearson, who used to be technical manager at Lawson's." Or, if they did, they were not going to work it out. They were not going to think or imagine that it was because I had sold my car and had no money that I stood there.

I would not have worn those clothes, which I used for interviews, if I had not been after a job that morning. It was normal that I should be looking for work. On fine mornings, I would walk down. It was a mile and a half from our house on Derrington Drive to the centre, and on the good days, when I told myself that the exercise gave me a sensation of well-being, I would think how fortunate I was. Nigel and Stephanie were off our hands and grown up, so that there was only Margaret and myself to consider. There were other things too, if I thought of them; and we still had the house. It had usually worn off by lunchtime.

Now my mind was on the interview, and I thought of the effect of knowing Fred Talbot. It had not helped. Maybe he thought I knew him too well.

I was standing in the doorway of Monsen's electrical shop, looking at the goods on display. I went in. Margaret's vacuum cleaner had broken down and there was a cut-price one in the window. I could not afford to buy it, but the rain started to stream down and the doorway became crowded. I went in to waste time.

I was served by a salesman at the counter. It was dry in the shop. While he got the vacuum cleaner and showed me, I looked at a girl in the back of the shop, only half listening. She was dusting stock, bending over an array of radiators they had on the floor. She was young and wore a mini-skirt and tights and had long legs. There was a flash of pink every time she bent down. It held my eye; I do not think it was more than that. When the salesman paused in his story, I said, "It looks like a cheap kind of plastic." He went on with his sales talk.

The girl turned and, looking over her shoulder, saw me gazing interestedly at her bottom. She looked at me, I looked at her. It was inexplicable, the moment's confusion. I said to the salesman, "I'll take it."

It was panic, for no reason, and I tried to recover myself. I could not afford that vacuum cleaner. It was not my fault that the girl wore pink knickers.

I had the money to buy it in the bank, but that did not mean a thing. What was in the bank, within the limit of my overdraft, was there in final reserve for the next mortgage payment. We lived and ruled our lives by our mortgage. I could not afford money.

"Yes, sir!" The salesman gave me a look of surprise. He had been working hard. He had been guessing the age of my wife and saying, yes sir; but lightness could be an advantage when you looked at it for the rather-more-older person.

I thought, What am I doing? and though I addressed the question to myself, after a year's unemployment I did not get any answer.

The girl gave me a look. She was about seventeen, and the look said, Dirty old man; somehow it hurt me. She put her nose in the air and went off round the shop. I could do nothing about the girl and I was stuck with the vacuum cleaner.

"Wait a minute," I said to the salesman. "Does the price include all the fittings?" But it did, and they were all in the box. He showed me and put the vacuum cleaner in its box. He was smiling, and I wondered unreasonably if they made sales that way, though I knew that they could not. He said, taking a look at me, "You'll be paying by cheque, sir?"

"Yes," I said. And there was nothing for it but to take out my cheque book. He let me start writing it in the way that they do, and then he said, "If you will put your name and address on the back, sir." I felt indignant. The cheque was all right, it was my bank account that was not. But I wrote, Dalby Pearson, 26 Derrington Drive, on the back. He watched me, and said, "You'll be taking this in your car, sir?" and he handed me the box by its handle.

If I had not been too busy feeling indignant, I would have demanded delivery and told him the truth: I had no car. The fact was, taking the cleaner in its box and heading for the glass door, I only wanted to get out and start thinking. Whatever it was I had done, I had done it.

The rain had stopped, and I could see that as I came to the door: there were no more people sheltering in the entrance. I opened the door and found myself among the usual housewives with shopping baskets at the lower end of the High Street. Then I started to think about my situation. I saw how unlike me it was, and how badly I had handled things. I was there in the High Street again, but with a vacuum cleaner in my hand that somehow had to be

9

explained to Margaret, with the mortgage payment impending.

I walked on up the High Street. I walked past most of the main shops; the same shops that you will find in any other small town, and they had all the same names above the windows. Lockley had been an individual town and had character when I was a boy. It had character now, in the way that the street bent, and the pavements were crowded in the post-lunch-time rush-hour, and the traffic was snarled up.

I had to walk until I could think of what to tell Margaret. Margaret, I convinced myself, was not difficult to explain to. Here is a present for you, dear, I imagined as I walked on up the High Street. It is a vacuum cleaner to clean the house with, but now I have bought it we will have to sell the house, and so you won't need to clean it. I could not see Margaret accepting that, not without comment, and not even with the best will.

I looked around me and decided to go to the park. As for the vacuum cleaner, I did not want to be wasteful and dump it.

The Lockley park was not big, and it was accessible by two side-streets of solicitors' offices. Recently, for a year, I had quite often gone there. There were the usual mothers with prams and children. The grass looked wet, but the people had come back. It just meant that the benches were occupied because the grass was too wet for the children to play on. Three boys were damaging trees on the far side. I looked for some place to stop, and was surprised to see one by an old man on a bench by the duck pond.

I was there strictly for thinking. It was not just a matter of jokes about Margaret. I put the box in the middle of the seat, like a barrier between us. The old man had sharp eyes.

"A vacuum cleaner. Are you one of those salesmen?"

I said "No," and I hoped that would hold him.

I had to think. I had to decide what to do or to say. On both subjects I appeared to have a completely blank mind.

It seemed to me that this was evidence of the same kind of incapacity I had felt in the shop. I could see it was the corrosive effect of a year's unemployment. Worse, it could be because I was fifty. The half century was half way to somewhere. That was even more irremediable.

I did not want to think of Fred Talbot that morning. It was quite evident that it was singularly useless.

"Why, Dalby," he said when he saw it was me he was interviewing, though he had my name in his file. "You know I can't take you on for this kind of thing. You know it's virtually labouring and leg-work. It would not be a kindness."

He could not take on the ex-technical manager of Lee and Lawson's Manufacturing Industries for labouring and leg-work. At least not in Lockley. His opinion had been shared.

I wondered what would be a kindness. What had he in mind? I thought it was probably what they did with old pets at the vet's. I did not think that that would be entirely unwelcome.

"It's a pity about the ducks," the old-age pensioner at the other end of my seat said.

I looked at him across the vacuum cleaner box, which was an inadequate fortification. It was not that I disliked talking to old-age pensioners as people. It was as a class I disliked them. Old-age pensioners were not expected to work. They were sixty-five and over. I was expected to work. For the next fifteen years. The expectation was never voiced, it was there. When Unemployment Insurance ran out, you got Social Security. Old-age pensioners were above that. They were a higher class of people. I just wished I could get work.

"What about the ducks?" I said civilly.

He looked knowing and pointed. He looked at the duck pond where I had been looking. It should have been obvious. He told me, "There are none."

I looked at the duck pond again. I had been staring at it. There always had been ducks on the duck pond at Lockley, the ornamental variety, and usually the seat we were on was occupied by young mothers with children, or old women with brown-paper bags. But that day there were none. There were neither the lonely old ladies, nor the children, nor the ducks.

"What happened to the ducks?"

He had won me. It was something I had to know. He had got my attention. It was as though I already knew.

"The vandals stoned them."

"Oh."

"Last night," he said, and he watched me.

"For God's sake," I said, and I felt it.

"For a giggle," he said.

"What?"

"That's what they said. The policeman saw them too late, but he caught one."

"Youngsters? Young people?"

He looked me over. I was only fifty. I was almost a young person myself, compared to him. I was young enough anyway to be in the class of their parents.

He said, "It's what they let them get away with."

We both looked over at the other side of the park where the boys were breaking the trees down.

I remembered a night in the week after we had had the telephone taken out because we could no longer afford it. Margaret had never been ill in the night all the time we had had the 'phone, but that night she was. Perhaps it was cause and effect. She had never been off the 'phone, ever. I went out, and because it was after midnight and the neighbours' lights were out, I went on down to the booth on the corner. When you needed a 'phone you could not have one. I saw the glass, glittering in the street before I got to the booth, little lights in the light of the street lamp.

Over on the other side of the park, one youth had jumped up and caught the branch of a tree. When he was on it, the branch was lower, and the others too could jump up and catch it. All three of them swung on the branch, lifting up their feet as it got lower. If you went and said anything to them, they were just playing. But anyone who knew boys knew they would not leave that branch until they broke it. Then they would look at it accusingly as though it had done something to them, and go out of the park, or more likely move on to the next one. I wondered if it were true, what the old man said: that it was what they found they could get away with. All people.

I got up and left the old man, I recognized the accusing tone of voice in which he said what he said. I took my vacuum cleaner with me. I was not going to get into that kind of an argument at that time. I looked around the park to see if there were anywhere else to sit, and when I found there was not I went off to the gate, and left it.

At the gate, I discovered there was nowhere for me to go but home. I had intended to go on the bus with the vacuum cleaner, but I decided to walk. It would take that much longer, and I had not done any thinking.

I looked at the streets and the houses and the shops as I walked out of town. What people could get away with, I thought. Such as enclosing every square inch of Lockley, and saying it was their town, and it was they, and not I, who was owner. It had never struck me before quite so forcibly how they got away with that, and with their ownership of what Karl Marx called the means of production.

What people could get away with, I thought.

I was ready for a rest by the time I had walked the long road out of town, but I toiled up the hill on the main road. I did not stop just anywhere, for I had no intention of looking distressed by the roadside like a hitch-hiker cadging a lift from the neighbours. I found a wall, and lifted the vacuum cleaner upon it. I balanced it with one hand. It was something of what I was trying to get at, as I looked down at that view.

The quiet hills that lay around the town, unlike the one I was on, were mostly bald-headed. On my right, looking down to the south, I could see Lee and Lawson's factory, on the river flats as we called it. Ramsden Bottom, not far from it, where I was born, had its quaint streets and mean roofs. The business section of Lockley made a noticeable centre. All the rest, with the exception of the parish church, was a sprawl, just residential streets and suburbs.

Standing there, I just hoped to rest my arms. I had no desire to review my life. I was not off on that tack.

All the same, some thoughts did come. Such as what had made me, a Ramsden Bottom boy, even after Grammar School, enlist in the army in wartime. Anti-Fascist? Hardly. But I could have got deferment, or gone into defence production. Excitement, I thought. Not setting out to defend the town, but finding a good excuse to leave it. Something of a joke, since I came through and came back, and the war made me as nothing else could. I came back a captain; but I in no way deserved it.

If it had not been for that temporary officer status, I could never have met Margaret. Looking across the valley, I could not see if that had been a good or a bad thing. More to the point, I would never have got the job with Lawson either. Or, if I had got a job, as a hand, I would not have stepped in on the staff. Technical manager, Royal Engineers background. That, too, was a bit of a joke, in a post-war Nissen-hut factory. But I was keen then to come back to Lockley.

I had parents. Some people got inheritances from their parents. I got responsibilities and a sick father who had given Lockley his best years. I could have filled in a form and gone to university, ex-officers' careers. I did not think a great deal about it. After the war, I did not object to being needed at home. My father's death reduced my yoke, my stint to my parents. Then mother got the widows' pension. I had wanted to go to the local tech to qualify, not like an officer, but we were working six nights a week at the time of expansion.

Looking down among the modern factories on the river flats, it was not easy to visualize it as it was when we were in the old Nissen huts and there was just myself and Lawson and twenty skilled and semi-skilled men. I could remember Lawson saying to me, "I'll see you all right." He was not quite an old bastard, was Lawson, now departed. He had had sense of some kind.

I looked to the north of the town, where, to the outrage of Margaret's people, she and I had first lived in a semi. That was the time the first factory went up. "It is all right," Margaret told her people. "You can see how they are expanding. Dalby will get there. It is only for a few years."

I shifted my gaze to Ramsden Bottom, and thought of taking Margaret back there, to my parents' old slum, as an unemployed man's wife. It was not on.

It had to be on. It was where unemployed men lived. Who did I think I was? I was an unemployment statistic. I had a Social Security number. National assistance was to be my state.

I looked at the rooftops of the Ramsden Bottom houses. We could buy our own house in the slum. That was what it meant, what we had saved on the Derrington Drive house. Then we would not get the rent allowance the other unemployed got. I tried to imagine Margaret in Ramsden Bottom, but I could not. Some things went too far. It was the shape of the roof-tops.

Blame? I wanted to blame Lawson. Or Lee. Or the soulless impersonal consortium that had taken over when Lawson, not Lee, died. "I'll see you all right," Lawson had said, but he had died, and there were twenty years between that and the consortium that now ran the factories on the far side of the houses.

The man to blame was Lawson's nephew, who inherited, and who was now living on a thirty-ton yacht with a girl on the Mediterranean at Portofino in Italy. If I had had that, at twenty-six, would I have come back to the rain and the smoke? Not these days. I faced it.

But the facts were the facts. It had happened. The man from the consortium's London office had taken over in Lockley.

'What do you know about computers, Mr Pearson?'

Time-and-motion study was about my level.

I looked down at the factory on the river flats. They had new young men now who ran it. They were college-trained and they cut one another's throats with new management techniques. Automation. Six weeks after they took over, the works stopped for three months. But they would iron out the snags. They would have to. They would find out in practice, as I had. I was out of date; out of date, by their standards.

Who was I kidding? It had just been my pride. I should have taken that foreman's job in Coventry when they offered. It had looked incredible at the time, including going to the midlands from Lockley. I had had the idea that it was I who put that factory there, the largest in Lockley. As Karl Marx said, it is simple. Get it into your head that someone else owns the means of production.

I was stuck there, balancing a vacuum cleaner on a wall by the main road.

Then I made up my mind. It was not easy. Was it pride? I did not think so. I picked up the vacuum cleaner, that I could have dropped over the wall, and took it home to Margaret.

Derrington Drive started at the top of the hill, branching off where the main road took a bend through the screen of the woods. The Misses Cleveland lived at number eighteen, Roger Belfont's was one of the larger of the white architect-designed houses in neat lawns. I wondered if it was right, what I was going to say, what I intended to do. The McFarlanes, the old retired couple, lived at number twenty-eight just beyond me. I turned in at my own gate.

I knew that Margaret would come to meet me, to hear if I had got the job, of which we had hopes, as soon as I came in at the front door.

It is not losing his job that affects a man so much. It is what he tells his wife, then and each time he fails to get a new one. Men can take many things that are very much worse than being unemployed; this was one. It was bright in the hall of our nice house, and I was taking my coat off between the castor-oil plant and the flowering cactus when she came into the hall from the kitchen. Firm-faced and ready for disappointment, she was already saying, "Dalby——?" when she saw what I had put on the floor. There was an illustration of the contents on the box, and the hose and the nozzle of the vacuum cleaner in the picture looked a little like a snake, and, taken-aback, she looked at it as though it were one.

A little wondering, not knowing why it was there, and not understanding anyway, she said, "Dalby, have you bought that?"

I went on taking off my coat and putting it away in the nice neat cupboard while she waited. I turned to her and smiled.

"I got a job," I told her. It was not quite my first lie.

2

LIKE ANY OTHER husband, I had lied to Margaret quite
habitually. They were ordinary husband-lies, like stopping
off at the pub or just talking, and then saying I was kept at
the office. Lies of this kind came in a special mild class.
It had something to do with intentions.

Actual infidelities, and things really to lie about, had
been rather rare. There had been no very strong feeling of
principle behind this, such as righteousness about sex or
religion. The way I thought about it was more that when
we were both young it had been unnecessary, and since then
I had had more things to do. It seemed natural, and the way
that it happened. I shall have to say more about Margaret.

For the moment, I was just cautious about lying. I was
economical about things that might be disproved. A lot of
the things I said came out in that way.

"You mean you got it?" She looked up at once.

I saw too much relief on her face. "No. Not the job, a job."
I did not intend too much. I warned her at once. "It isn't a
good one."

It was the marriage situation. I looked at Margaret. We
had time to study one another's expressions.

They say all marriages are different. I was limited. I had
only known one. Margaret, then Margaret Kingsman, had
been a tall, shy, remote girl when I married her. I was sure
that time was the essence of marriage. It made women, quite
as much as their parents.

She still showed signs of her father's big house. But I mean
that a woman's life is more divided into halves than a

man's. Not that the house had been all that big, before she took her mad risk and threw in her lot with me and a semi against the warnings of her parents. Dog-and-gun was the way I thought of it, rather than horses and county, but then that was the point. I had never been clear, and still wasn't, about the social distinctions.

She looked at me with a particular expression that was as good as any words after twenty-five years.

Margaret was still gaunt. She was not the kind that ran to fat, but when she was present she was physically there. Her shyness and remoteness had become reserve. To most people she looked inexorable, and she was, even to me, except sometimes. The way she was looking at me was because I had said "a job", and repeated it three times, and not once said "employment", or "a position" or "work".

It may seen ridiculous that two people married twenty-five years, should still use different languages, and still notice they did, even in crises. It happened in crises precisely. We had our ideas of what was important.

Maybe it said something about both of us. It said something about me. I was resistant. That was because I was on the technical side, not the management side. Margaret was immutable. The most we could win was respect. Any weakness would be unconditional surrender.

Margaret stood on the far side of the vacuum cleaner and watched me as I watched her.

"If you have obtained work, that is the main thing."

She said "work" and not "employment" because I objected to words of ten letters. Who knew? We might meet in a concise English language someday. Between us, we might even change it.

All right, all physical love was past, but she was still the big event in my life.

"You should give me time to explain," I said.

"If it gives you time to look around."

"It's temporary." I told her the worst thing.

I had worked out some of the details coming along the Drive.

"Two evenings a week." I expanded. "When I said that it's not good, I mean it is part-time." I watched Margaret take her disappointment.

She thought of me.

"Dalby, is this something you must do?"

"Yes."

Together, in a unanimous way, we looked at the vacuum cleaner.

"It is pointless for you to earn if you spend it."

"I can't have you cleaning the house with a dustpan and brush."

"If that were all," she said darkly.

Then she looked at me sharply. "Did you have lunch?"

It was a matter about which we lied to one another.

"Of course." I saw her move, and stepped over the vacuum cleaner. There was no way out of that one.

It was by mutual consent. It was not only for Margaret. We were going to live for ever in the Derrington Drive house. What would we do if we sold up?

It was the way we were living. We could not economise on the rates, nor the mortgage, so we economised on food. These were not lies at all, since they came from both parties.

"I had my lunch early," she said.

We went through into our pleasant, spacious living-room. We had ceased to buy clothes, and we walked to save bus-fares, but everything in the living-room was intact. We were Derrington Drive people. I looked at the fire. I was seeking some distracting activity, and I went across to poke it.

I was wary. Margaret was beginning to get a grasp of things.

"How did you come to get this work, Dalby?"

"I met a man in a pub." The fire required coal.

"In a pub?"

She found it hard to believe that one.

"When the job I went for fell through, I invested in a glass of beer."

She said "Oh", unbelieving. I concentrated on the fire. We had central heating. Central heating and a fire. Only we could not afford to run the central heating. It was like eating. We did not freeze in the house. Only the water-pipes in winter. We kept the living-room fire alight with a few embers.

"It was in the Bull," I said, knowing that a place made for more credible fiction. I remembered something that once happened.

"I quietly drank a half, and there was a man complaining about his income-tax." I looked over my shoulder.

"Income-tax?"

"You've heard of it. Did you know I was an expert?"

"Dalby."

"Yes," I said, holding the fire-tongs. "I know."

She looked as troubled as I expected her to be. About Margaret I could forecast.

"He puts bills in his pocket and sends them to the laundry," I said. "Because he's a builder. So he can't produce his receipts for the income-tax. He once did some work for us at Lee and Lawson's." This character existed.

It had happened nine months ago, in the early days of my unemployment. I had not told Margaret then. When it had happened, and I had offered my services, as tax-consultant, Williams had said gloomily, "I have an accountant." He looked at me, after my offer of work, as though I were a pimp who had tried to sell him my sister.

Margaret had the illusion that people in business were more rational and at the same time more credulous.

"I offered to go to his house two nights a week," I said.

"Nights?" She looked as though I meant midnight.

"Evenings," I corrected. "Two evenings a week until he gets his books right. It's all right," I gave her an assurance. "At least I hope that it will be."

Margaret stood half way between the door from the hall and the one that was open to the kitchen. She was torn between listening, because she wanted to know and was doubtful, and going to get us the meal that was our substitute for lunch and that we called afternoon tea. At breakfast, we had toast and weak coffee. By three in the afternoon we had thin slices of bread and the tea cups. Our one meal of the day was called dinner, and we had that late in order to last out until bedtime.

She started for the kitchen, and came back.

"What about what you get from your Unemployment benefit?"

She did not call it the dole. Her husband would not be on the dole. But she knew that if I earned anything appreciable they would make deductions accordingly.

"I shan't tell them about it."

She thought. "Who is this builder?"

"Wether," I said positively. It was a name I chanced to know was not in the telephone directory. I also thought it best to set him away at a distance. "He has a small place at Conlea."

She looked. "I have never heard of a builder called Wether."

Then she went off to the kitchen to get me the afternoon tea.

Margaret's mind worked in two stages. First she absorbed facts. Then some worry set in. After getting facts, she applied her high principles to them. I sat there and waited.

"Dalby!" she said from the kitchen.

"Yes," I said.

"How can you not tell the Social Insurance about your part-time work?"

"I'll just not tell them."

She appeared in the doorway.

Margaret had a sense of rectitude. Perhaps it was more a feeling of righteousness. It was what her pride had become. She had not moved with the times. She had not wanted to move with the times. She even looked, sometimes, like something from a past age; but that was a deliberate contrivance.

"You can't do it and not tell them." she said. "It would be just the same as stealing."

"Yes," I said.

"You can't do it," she said as though I had not got the point.

"Why not?" I said. I put on my philosophic and didactic expression and looked straight at her. "All other moral values are being questioned these days, so why should we not question that one?"

She looked nonplussed. She liked to be modern. As well. She did not know whether to go back into the kitchen or stay where she was.

She said, "Dalby, that isn't like you."

I knew that my own attitude to her was equivocal, but I could not help it.

"I know," I said. "But I have become embittered."

She looked alarmed. "It won't do," she said, and went back into the kitchen.

I was surprised. It seemed that I was succeeding. I sat there reflecting.

I wished I did know what I felt about Margaret. I loved her. It was certainly not sex. Sex had ceased. In any event, I had long ago come to the conclusion that sex with a wife was over-rated. Secretly, I had once thought it was like making love to your sister. It was just that she was there; and I was, at the same time, afraid of that force of character that had enabled her to marry me; it was at odds with, and, in the same instant respectful of, her old-time standards. My sex life, when I thought of it, was not getting anywhere either. Perhaps it should not, at fifty.

Margaret came back. It was not exactly to attack. She carried a tray with our tea, cups and plates, on each of which was a small spoonful of jam, and the thin bread. Very refined,

23

but I could see from her eyes she had found a gap in my story.

"Dalby, how do you expect to get back from Conlea?"

Perhaps I had chosen Conlea unwisely.

"Oh." I was cautious. "I expect that I'll get back."

"Not now they've cut the buses." They were cutting the bus service recklessly now that all people had cars. "The last back is half past eight, except, I think, on Fridays."

I thought. Well, I had already half decided.

I would need, I imagined, some transport of some sort.

"I shall go on Nigel's bicycle."

She did not drop the tray. She just looked.

"You, on a bicycle."

"Why not? I can."

"At your age."

I did not think my age important.

"You never forget how to ride one."

She spoke with some satisfaction, in demolishing both husband and income, and with total illogic. "You will end up dead under a bus."

She did not express any regret, and I thought about marriage.

I could make demands too. I had one demand to make, and I slipped it in at what I hoped was the right time.

"Since I am not working officially," I said, "for the Unemployment benefit..." she looked and I continued "... you must not tell the neighbours."

"On a bicycle," she said. "And it's coming on to winter."

3

I DO NOT know if I would have kept to my decision if it had not been for my story, about Mr Wether employing me.

I think not. I could not go at once. Nigel's bicycle had been hung in the garage, since he went to Australia, about two years. I had to go into the town and get lights and batteries and take the week-end to repair it.

"When do you start?" Margaret said when she came out to watch me.

I said, "Tuesday."

Those thoughts, about other people owning all the buildings of Lockley, all the offices and factories, the shops, all the fields in the landscape, all the means of production; they were true of course. Property was not a divine right. I was born there, and had as much right to work as them, or more in most cases. I looked out over the town from the bedroom.

But facts grow dim when you have lived with them for fifty years and done nothing about them. Sometimes, I was aware, if you could call a fact "political" it ceased to be a fact at all.

The real fact was, I was committed. Besides, I had to pay for the vacuum cleaner.

On a dry autumn evening, I took Nigel's bicycle out of the garage after darkness. I looked at the leaf-patterns and the lights of the street lamps along the Drive. Mrs Peverley was going into her garden, and I waited. When she had gone, and I wheeled the bicycle out to the gate, I heard a clatter from the McFarlanes. He was filling his coal bucket. What did I expect? No one could be invisible in Lockley. Maybe he had not seen. I got on the bicycle and wobbled down the Drive.

It was true you did not forget, but I would have done better to practise. Because of my intentions, I had not liked to advertise myself in the daytime. I turned the corner in the dark. I was passed by a bus on the main road. I headed for the northern suburb. It was easy down the hill on the bicycle. The bicycle had been partly an accident, forced on me by Margaret's ideas, but it was useful as transport, and easier to hide than a car. Probably a little more conspicuous than walking. At the bottom of the hill, I turned left and rode around the by-pass in the evening traffic in the usual way. As soon as I got to the northern suburb, I left the by-pass and got off the bicycle and parked it.

Even a bicycle requires a little care if it is to be hidden, and not arouse questions in someone's mind. On that first night, I had everything planned and knew just where I was going. I parked the bicycle behind an electricity transformer sub-station that stood under some trees in a little triangle of land among the houses of the suburb. I looked very carefully along the street to see if anyone were watching me when I put it in, and I did the same when I came out. I was under no illusions, and my business was serious.

The public generally assume that burglary is committed by gay stop-at-nothing desperadoes, by gentlemen who do not really intend to steal for money, by vicious crooks, or by rugged stupid people who have a heart of gold under their ex-boxer exteriors. Burglary is not commonly done by these people. It is performed unsuccessfully by tramps, and successfully by sneak-thieves; which is what I was, or would be.

The best time to operate, I had decided, was from about eight p.m. onwards. People who were going out for the evening in Lockley would invariably be out by eight. They were very regular in their habits. I was lucky it was autumn, for I was able to tell who was in and who was out by the lights in the houses.

I walked the streets inconspicuously in the suburb. I had to choose my house properly, and I had still some things to learn. I neither hastened nor loitered, and I examined each house with a glance as I came to it. I took time choosing a house, but when I did, I only paused long enough at its gate as though to glance at its number.

The road was empty, I was not seen, and I went to the front door. I looked for reflections of light from the back as I approached, then put my hand to the bell. I stood back from the front door and looked at the shadows of the garden. I looked at the windows of the houses across the street to see if I could see any faces. It was all quite natural, for a man who was waiting. I found I had talent.

I went round the back of the house. I first made sure there were no lights, even faint ones. I examined the neighbours' gardens in the reflection of their lights. Then I made myself inconspicuous and tried the back door and back windows of the house. I was unsuccessful, for they were all firmly locked. I thought, what do I do now? I looked for a key under the back door mat.

Any intelligent person would know that a burglar had to try a number of houses.

I went on through the suburb. The people I called on were out. I did not enter the garden of more than one house in any one street. I was not trying houses. I was a respectable citizen who was calling on friends. Better still, I was not there, and not noticed.

There was a house that was more successful. It was detached and old-fashioned, and I chose it for that reason. It was straggling, with a not-too-well-kept, slightly damp look. It also had high hedges, good shadows, and a shed in the garden. I had been careful to wear gloves. It was something I did know; and I opened the shed first. I found a spade. There were other tools, but a spade was the best tool for a burglar.

It was the fact that it had a full-length, wooden-framed

French window in an alcove at the back that made me decide upon the house. Perhaps it was true I had talent at last and found I was doing the right thing. Doors with thin wooden frames could only be secured by small bolts and relatively small screws. Besides, the woodwork was damp, and I decided it would come open if I inserted the spade between the two halves of the door. I was cautious in case I fractured the glass, and put the spade in the right places.

I put the spade down and looked and listened. It had been dangerously easy.

I entered. This was it. The unknown dark room had unexpected obstacles of strange furniture, and I went through it, to the inner door, keeping my torch beam low. I remembered that burglars were sometimes caught because flashing lights were seen in what were otherwise empty houses. I thought fairly steadily about how burglars were caught. I did not waste time, but I knew I had my retreat still open. It seemed to me that I had a thing to do, and I went right through the house and slid the bolt on the front door.

I wanted time to get away, out of the dark house if necessary, and I guessed that if anyone came home and tried to go in with a key, and found the front door would not open, they would think it jammed. They would spend time fussing and pushing at it. The same applied to the back door, and I went and locked that too. It seemed to me that I was the one with the interior lines of communication. So I was better with the doors locked. I was the one who could unlock them, and choose which of the ways I went out. I could not lock the French window.

It had not seemed possible to me that I could think of the ethics of what I was doing while I was doing it, but I did. I noticed the property in the house. There were book-cases and a cabinet of cups of some kind. They could have been valuable, but I did not take them.

In some way that was suitable to me, to my particular mind, morals, and the need that Margaret and I had, that

I had to relieve, seemed to go together. I was not there to make a big haul. I wanted money, and not even that in large quantities, and I set out to look for it. I was clear about one thing. There was another way that burglars were caught, and I was not going to leave the house with anything that could be identified as not my property later.

It took time, and more time than I expected, to look for money in a house. Later it was quicker, but at first I did not know where to find it. I wondered, upstairs or down? I tried downstairs first, since it seemed dangerous to go so far from the doors as to go upstairs, but that was a waste of time in that house. The sideboard drawer was fruitless. Downstairs, I drew a blank except for some change that had probably been left out for the milkman. If I had found any more, I would not have gone upstairs.

I did not know that the front best bedroom, with the marital bed, was the best place to find money in any house. I got there by accident. It was lighted by the reflection of the street lamps, and I could see the gate and the street from the window. Maybe it was that which made me spend more time there. I felt the money in a small soft handbag under the clothes in a woman's drawer. I did not know how much it was. It felt like something between thirty and fifty.

Why was it there? Maybe she thought that her husband would be knocked down in the street someday. Maybe there was something, a secret from him, for which she was saving. I wondered, standing by the bed, looking at the street and putting the money in my wallet. Later, I learned that the front best bedroom was always the surest bet. Sometimes it could be found in the pocket of a man's suit. Maybe she was saving for a divorce.

I wondered if she would tell him it was gone, if he did not know she had it. Then I thought of the door I had broken. She would tell him. Someday I would learn how to get into a house without leaving any sign, but I was not yet at that stage.

I turned and looked at the jewelry on her dressing table. It was what the police would expect me to take, and then they could notify all the second-hand dealers and keep a watch on the fences. It was not even valuable, to be left out like that.

I had to think in terms of self-preservation. I would be mad to become an identifiable thief who only took money. I picked up the jewelry and wondered if I could bury it in the garden. I had a better idea than that. There was a lavatory at the end of the passage, and, using my torch, I took the jewelry and wrapped each piece separately in toilet paper, and flushed it.

Then I went out. I went out the same way I had come in. I went round first, and unbolted the doors. I even pulled the French window to. I knew that to look like a regular thief I ought to throw out the contents of drawers, and break a few things, and perhaps urinate on the carpet, and leave a disorder; but I did not feel like that on that night.

I never did feel like that. I always told myself I ought to create unnecessary damage, but I never did. It was stupid and dangerous. It must surely have given the police a lead on me, and enabled them to say which crimes were mine. I should have followed the normal practice of a regular revengeful thief in every way, yet I was obstinate. The police were not going to catch me anyway. To do it, they would have had to be there when I went into a house, and I always saw that they were not. I did not want revenge. I had been as thoughtless about the unemployed as anyone else when I had been technical manager at Lee and Lawson's. I only wanted payment, compensation.

When I came out of the house, I went round the side and stood in the shadows while I looked at the front. I looked at the nearby houses to see that I was not seen. Then I went to the gate, and took a look at the street to see there was no one there, and walked out.

Instants after I had left the gate, I was an ordinary respectable citizen walking down the street on legitimate business. They could have stopped me and questioned me and searched me then and there. They might have had their suspicions but they could not prove anything. The money in my wallet was my own. It was up to them to prove otherwise if they denied it.

It is difficult to tell exactly what I felt at that time.

I knew it would not last. It was just the having done it, and being out and away, and the relief from tension. There was a background too. A year applying for jobs and being turned down was one thing. The clerks at the Employment Exchange, and other people too were responsible, not wittingly, not deliberately, and yet in some way. Do this and do that. I am afraid we have to know exactly what you have, Mr Pearson. It is the regulations you see. You understand, I am quite sure, that we have to fill in this form correctly. It had hurt me, with my background.

It was a matter of money, not having money. I had money in my pocket again as I walked those streets back to the bicycle. I already knew, though I pretended I had not decided in my mind, that I would do it again and could get more. It was said, and I had always believed it, that to be a thief was a mean and despicable thing. It was low, it destroyed your self-respect, and it was most of all demeaning. I felt it in just the reverse of that way.

I could have wept. If I did, it was not over what I had become, it was more with relief and self-justification and pride. There were reasons. I believe it was a virility thing. I was going home with money in my pocket for the first time in a year. It was not money that had been given to me, but got by own efforts and with a little risk. I went back to the bicycle and took it from where I had hidden it, and looked at the street and mounted it in a deliberate way. It would not last, but I was me again for the time being. There were such things as morals and ethics, but they were not what I felt. In myself, in the circumstances, I did not believe that what I had done could be in any way called a bad thing. It was, on the contrary, the one justifiable and appropriate line of conduct for any unemployed man, whom the community had locked out.

4

I WISH IT had been so simple. If, for example, other people had thought as I did. Then there would have been no complications. From Margaret, for instance.

I will have to recount some aspects of my life as a burglar.

It is probably easy to claim I was special, but I am not so sure that I was. I do not want to set up the idea that I was specially privileged—by my family circumstances for example, or because I was formerly respectable—until I was "forced into crime", and that I then only stole for Margaret. This may even have been true, but even if it were true of my first crimes, it would be wrong in that though those would be excuses, they would not be my excuses.

I did not think, at any time: This is all right for me, but it would not be right for other people. If I had thought that I was specially privileged, and if I had envisaged a wigged barrister making a plea for me in a court (though in fact I did not), and saying that I had been unfortunate and unjustly treated, and that I only stole to keep my wife in the minimum standard to which she had always been accustomed, then I, like any other criminal, would equally have understood the reply that would have been made against me.

It would merely have seemed to me a part of the law's charade, like the counter-argument of the prosecuting counsel, or the judge in his robes when summing up or passing sentence. It was just because I was a respectable man, who had been responsible for so long, that I should have known better. As a professional man, I could in no way claim not to know what I was doing. I had a duty to uphold society, and because I had not, and because I had used what intelligence I had to my own advantage, I was therefore liable not to a lighter, but to a heavier sentence.

When I say that I was not special and that, on the contrary, I was like any other criminal, I mean that I did not think of all this at all. Like any other criminal, had I thought of all this, what I would have thought would have been that these arguments were just the way that lawyers made their money. In the mood I was in, I would have gone further. I would have said that the lawyers made their money in this way by battening on the misfortunes of other people. And so true was this that I think any other wrongdoer would see it the same way.

It was a matter of the language in which things were expressed. Lawyers, and courts, and people professionally engaged in justice, thought in terms of "offences" and "the section of the Act". Had I come before them, they would have talked about "the position of the accused", and "mitigating circumstances" or their absence, and "culpability". I came to realize later that even prisoners, even people condemned for murder, were so brain-washed by this language in the end that even they, murderers, sometimes came to believe in the death penalty. It was a matter of verbal battery, of the articulate assurance of the educated well-to-do, and their insistence that reality was the way they saw things. They were so clever in the way they put over their point of view in lengthy words, and so assured, that neither they, nor the public in the court, nor in the end even the prisoner in the dock, could believe that other people, ordinary people, did not think in these words.

Were words, the words people used when they spoke and thought, the image of the world they lived in? I know my words, and the ways in which I thought, were not very good, and often muddled, as the reader will have seen. But my words and muddled phrases, uncouth as they were, and coming from such a mixed and muddled background, did seem to me to apply to things as they were, and to the things that people did, and in a sense they explained the more realistic doings, and the feelings and fears and hopes, of more actual people. Maybe other criminals, and other prisoners or would-be prisoners before the law, also lived in their worlds, and used the language they happened to speak, and it was nothing like the lawyers'. And in that case nothing was more true than that someone, somewhere, was not talking or thinking about the world as it was, but about their own created fiction.

It was the first time I had thought about reality. I am not sure that at that time I knew I thought of things like that, and it was more a feeling that I was going to have to do some thinking.

5

I AWOKE. TWIN beds, and the other bed was empty.

Something had happened. I was aware of it on waking, before I knew if it were good or bad. It was the morning after my first night out on Mr Wether's employment. I looked at the faint light around our heavy curtains.

I am a burglar. It came to me clearly. If I were caught. I thought of the effects on my family. I wondered for an instant whether I should leap up and put on my trousers in case the police came to get me. It would be ridiculous to be interviewed without trousers. I did not take any action on that thought. I was fifty, not fifteen.

What I knew was that my mood of elation of the night before had not lasted through the day's awakening. Such a mood never did last. But it was replaced by something different, more sober and cautious, but not wholly unlike it. It was the ordinariness of the ordinary criminal's life. I saw that. The difference was, I was the criminal. That was a new thing.

In my mind, I went quickly over the events of the previous night. I had not made any mistakes that I knew of. The police were not miracle workers. It was arguable, by other people, whether what I had done was justifiable. What I felt as I awakened was relief that today was not hopeless like yesterday.

I lay for a while. I thought I would go on trying for jobs. I was not wholly sold on crime. I believed that I saw it as a temporary expedient. At least, that was what I told myself the first morning. I did not live up to it very much even then.

Margaret had not been in the habit of getting up to make my breakfast. It was something done specially because I was back at work. I thought about that too. Was it because I was working, or because I had been out late the previous night, or had I overslept? I checked the time. It was the time I used to get up when I went to Lee and Lawson's. She used to make my breakfast then, and had only stopped when I finished work. Recently we had been in the habit of staying in bed late to save the coal that the fire took. It seemed I was virtuous. It was because I was working. If I worked, then she did the housework. When I listened, I could hear a clatter of cups in the kitchen. I wondered if burglary were the equivalent of honest work, and a journey to Conlea.

Five minutes later, I heard the kitchen door, and she came to the foot of the stairs. "Dalby! Are you up, or shall I bring you a cup of tea?" I elected to have a cup of tea. I called down to her, and she brought it up; I drank it in bed, with mixed feelings. It was unusual that first day. Before long, it would be routine that I would go out on Tuesdays and Fridays, and then, when my cup of tea in bed was expected, I became fretful if it was late. I discovered that a burglar's life was like any other.

After I had had my tea that day, I got up and went to the bathroom and dressed to go out. I had to go out to the bank to replace what I had spent on the vacuum cleaner. Another surprise awaited me at breakfast. Somehow, and presumably because work entitled me to it, I was given an egg. I noticed that Margaret restricted herself to the same old toast. "You must do an egg for yourself, too," I said. I was aware of the money in my wallet. "We can afford it."

I felt a wholly unusual pleasure in telling Margaret that she could go back to eating. I do not know what distress my burglary of the house with the insecure French window caused, but I was sure that it was counter-balanced by my feelings of quite simple pleasure at being able to tell Margaret that she, too, could have an egg. If there are to be any moral precepts, to replace the "ethical systems" and the quite extraordinary nonsense that one hears sometimes on the radio from lawyers and professors, I could not help feeling that it would have to be by some system of values that was run on this basis. For an egg for your wife, how do you stop crime?

Unfortunately, like anyone else who has had a "conversion", I could not resist the temptation to proselytize. There could hardly have been more unrewarding ground on which to sow the seed than Margaret at breakfast time.

"Dalby, has your Mr Wether told you how much he will pay you?"

"He gave me £5 that he said were for expenses."

"Is that all?"

"No, I am to get commission. Commission on what I save him on income-tax." I invented.

"I don't understand."

"I think it is an incentive bonus system, dear, to get me to cook his books without his knowledge. Do you think that I should?"

"No," said Margaret.

I could see it was going to be difficult to get someone like Margaret to compromise with her morals. I could see equally that it did not matter what the morals were, or whether they were just or not. She would rather suffer very great pangs than tamper with an established system. She came back to the attack. She put on a suffering expression for a long time after I had suggested that I might compromise the truth of Mr Wether's books, even though he was willing.

"I am not sure I can accept this, Dalby," she suddenly burst out. "You are getting your unemployment pay by false pretences. It is not like you, and I don't think I can stand it."

She did not say quite what she was going to do about it. I wondered if she would say she would leave me, but she did not.

I admired Margaret. De-sexed as she had become, I felt sure

that she had a force of character that would have led her to starve, literally, rather than leave Derrington Drive. After all, she had, and I had shared her starvation with her. It did cross my mind, though not with any meaning until long afterwards, that crime was necessarily a sign of weakness.

All this was a part of my lying to Margaret. I was now, already, lying to her by particularly advanced implications, and I was not sure why I wanted to "involve" her. It was a project entered into without sufficient thought, and as a part of what could only be called my "new style".

"It will be convenient," I said, "if we can afford things like new towels for the bathroom. You have often said so, dear."

"The towels we have will do."

"Not if we have a visit from your cousin Mavis, or any of the Kingsmans. You remember you said it was because of the towels you could no longer invite cousin Mavis."

"Part-time book-keeping is bad enough, Dalby. But if you are doing any of the things you are talking of now, I could not possibly have any of my family come here."

In case, presumably, I thought, there were some "difficulty with the police" while they were here. Perhaps that was why I wanted to involve Margaret, and make her, unnecessarily but in a mild way, share my own anxiety.

I did not resent Margaret's family, or her attitude to them, but I was aware of them, and of such people as her highly respected and esteemed Kingsman uncle in the background, who had gone to London and become "something in the City" on a large scale. He was in fact, as I knew, involved in company law and finance, and, septuagenarian and doddering on the point of retirement as he was, he had, ever since the consortium took over Lee and Lawson's, come into the category of "the enemy". He was more so now.

I did not do any more to subvert Margaret's moral rectitude that day, but went out to the bank. Before I left the house I went out to the garage, saying that I had to look to see if I needed something to repair the bicycle. What I did was to look around our outwardly elegant but inwardly empty and spider-inhabited garage until I found a tin box, I divided the money from my wallet and put half in the tin box, which I hid in a corner among spiders' webs, where I knew Margaret would never find it. It was necessary to have two accounts going now, it seemed to me, one in the bank and the other in the tin box, while my wallet, at any time Margaret happened to chance across it, would bear inspection.

The clerks at the bank were not likely to pay much interest to the state of my account if it remained within what the manager had declared to be my overdraft limits. But it would not do for it suddenly to go healthily into the black. The amounts that were paid in had to be such as might be gained by an unemployed man living off the fat of his home, who went out and sold things.

I went down into the town on the bus, since it had come on to rain, and gazing out at the streets of Lockley I noticed for the first time how people had come to look a little different. I do not believe I had really noticed pedestrians in the street and people in cars before. I was astonished at their dress and their busy, and apparently compulsive, ant-like behaviour. It struck me that they would have looked just as busy, and just as sure that what they were doing was right, if they had been born as peasants in China, among the Aztecs, or as citizens of Rome during the ancient empire. They were so obviously immersed in, and preoccupied with, all the details of life, as it happened to be at that time in Lockley. I had not felt so separate and apart from other people before.

I noticed that my bank had a marble exterior and an interior that was vaguely church-like. For some inexplicable reason, as I waited in the queue to the counter, I looked at the self-absorbed people who were also there and thought of the story of Christ cleansing the temple of the money-changers. Now we virtually built temples to money, and they were far more numerous than the other kind. I did not know why I, of all people, should feel my own sense of rectitude, so different from Margaret's, on that particular morning. I could only guess it was an attempt to establish my own righteousness and my alternative system of virtue, since I had lost the conventional one. The reasonable criticism, of how Lockley lived, seemed wholly logical and justified and quite right to me, and yet it was only a defence of some kind.

What I did when I was not thinking, which was something I seemed to be doing more of than ever in my life before, was to look at the woman ahead of me in the queue, and guess that, since she carried a neat stiff white-plastic shopping bag, she was just a housewife who had come in to cash her husband's cheque. I placed myself behind her in the queue because I believed that, unlike the other business people, she would not delay me. When she got to the counter, she too produced piles of money out of her bag and a shop-keeper's pay-in book, and bags of change, some of which the clerk emptied out and re-counted. I looked over the shoulder of her coat and saw the name of the store, Peverills, on her book. I knew where it was, and I could visualize the route she must have followed to come to the bank. There must have been £400 in her transaction, in notes and small change, and so far as I could see she had trusted to her appearance as a housewife and had come without an escort. It struck me then that the proceeds of a money-snatch could be rewarding, and that by joining a bank-queue like that it would be easy to spot suitable victims. I discounted the idea for the present, however, for it seemed to me that burglary was quite suitable for my purposes, and as to daylight robbery, I would be sure to be spotted and recognized if I did anything of the kind in Lockley.

I have mentioned this day in detail because it was very similar in pattern to those that followed in the kind of things I did and thought about. The same was true when I came home at lunch-time. The rain had cleared away, as was its habit that season, and the autumn sun had come out. Old McFarlane was working in his garden sweeping up leaves, which was a steady occupation in Derrington Drive at that time of year. I had the parcel of food I was bringing home for Margaret under my arm, but I paused at my gate, which was adjacent to his, and said:

"Hello! You can do mine too if you like." I gestured at the weather. "It looks like a nice day."

"Hello, Pearson." He paused on his broom. He always was old-fashioned. But he said. "Was it you on a bicycle last night?"

I felt a spasm of alarm. I had no reason to be alarmed. At least not much. There was no law against riding a bicycle. But I was. Maybe it was a social thing. People in Derrington Drive did not ride bicycles. There were cars at all houses.

"It was me." I had to brazen it out. "I'm doing evening work. But don't tell anyone will you?"

Like hell he would. And why should he not tell?

He looked at me with surprise. "You don't want people to know?"

I thought quickly, smiling at him. What I had to do was to make up my mind whether to tell him and Margaret different stories or similar ones.

"I'm doing book-keeping, part-time, for a builder in Con-lea. You know how it is." I put on an interview-board voice. "'And what was your last employment, Mr Pearson?' I don't want to have to tell someone that my last work was working for a builder in a small way."

His eyes looked as though they understood only vaguely. He had lived a secure life with no disappointments. He had a pension and had nothing to do. He was interfering and an inveterate gossip, and the story of me riding a bicycle and working part-time for a builder was just the kind of story he would tell.

"I see," he said, though he did not.

I gave him up. I would have to accept it.

42

"How's Mary?" I asked.

"She has got over her cold." He prepared to tell me the exact stage she had got to. He was polite first. He asked me, "How's Margaret?"

"She hasn't got a cold yet." I waved and went in.

I spent some time worrying over things of that kind. It was pointless: I could do nothing about them. It was just that my imagination would work.

I could see McFarlane talking to someone at a green at the golf club. To make conversation, they would ask him what had happened to Pearson. He would say, "Working part-time, for a builder at Conlea."

"That's a bit odd," the other man would say, addressing the ball, "I didn't know there were any builders, of that kind, at Conlea."

Did people take up conversations of that kind?

But it was more the fact that I was practising burglary regularly, two nights a weeks, on Tuesdays and Fridays, that gave me a new outlook on life. A worm's-eye view you might say. I could do nothing about the fact that it was soon known that I went out on the bicycle on those nights, and they could read in the paper that the burglaries in Lockley took place on Tuesdays and Fridays, if ever they noticed. I had to rely on what I had noticed about people. If it had not been for human indifference the burglary would never have been needed.

6

IT DEVELOPED QUITE slowly. What happened were facts. They had not much to do, a lot of them, with my moral progression. Indifferent facts, and indifferent people. I made some mistakes with my burglary. I was in the same position as any other man learning a trade, and I had to. I could learn, but I did not know it to start with.

On a night when we had fog in late November, I tried the council estates. I had known for some time that I could not continue to go to the suburbs to the north of the town. That was the kind of mistake that burglars who were caught made; I thought about such mistakes and I was not going to make them.

The alternative was to try other, less wealthy suburbs, and in some of them, on the estates, the houses were more close-packed and more dangerous. The council houses were the worst, and when the night of the fog came along it seemed the best weather for that district. I was there, and in a small, narrow, low-fenced garden, protected only by the fog, which I thought was an advantage, when the dog started barking.

I did not like it because the house next door, where the dog was, was just over the fence; even through the fog I could see, by its lights, that it was occupied. I had chosen the garden I was in because it, and the semi-detached that it adjoined, had no lights. I had gone into the garden shed to get some means of entry, and had had more luck than I expected because I found a key; and that was important. The houses were too close together for me to risk the noise that might arise if I tried breaking and entry, and a key was a rare find.

Later, I discovered it was not as rare as all that. I was still in the state of pondering police advice to burglars—such as look for a key on a window-ledge, or under a mat. The police did not say that. They issued notices warning householders not to leave a key out in that way, under a flower-pot for example, but it came to the same thing. I lived in a more sophisticated generation. The people were more sophisticated than the police, I discovered, and they did not leave keys under mats like their parents. They hung them on nails just inside the door of the garden shed, where a child could reach them; and it was there, fumbling around in the dark, and attracting the attention of the next door's dog, that I found it.

At least I no longer thought burglary so remarkable that as soon as anything happened I had to cut and run. I was developing my own style as any craftsman. It was a small, interested and playful dog, and it would have been no trouble had we been in the same garden. I spoke to it over the fence. I did not want to leave, because I had found a key and there was the fog; but when I moved away it felt lonely and barked. I knew dogs lost interest when I went into a house. It was a Yale key and the back door had a Yale lock. I put the key in the door and tried it.

On a clear night, a householder took no notice when he heard his dog barking. He thought it had found a cat. He decided it was barking at another dog. That night was different. I had put the key in the door and turned it, when the neighbouring back door flew open and a man appeared in the light peering into the fog.

He said, "Prince! What is it, Prince boy?"

I was on the edge of the light and could not get the key out soundlessly. I took my hand away from it. The dog barked at me when encouraged by his owner. The man looked and said,

"What is it, Prince?"; then saw, and said, "Who are you?"

It was the first occasion I had been caught trying to make entry to a house, and I wondered what to do. I decided to keep my head about it.

"Hello," I said. "Can you tell me if Mrs Victoria lives here?"

"Mrs Victoria."

"Yes."

"No, there's no one here of that name."

He came to the fence to see me, but I stood with my face out of the light.

I did not want to make him suspicious, so I said, "42 Willoughby Avenue." I had the sense not to say "Crescent" for we were in the Crescent. I always looked at the streets and house numbers.

"This is Willoughby Crescent," he said as though I were dim. "You want two lower down for the Avenue."

Everything should have been all right then. I had it under control. I was saying "Thank you" and turning to go when there were footsteps, along the street, that slowed down and stopped. I could not see anyone. Then the gate clicked. The heavy footsteps started to approach and turned off to the front door, but then the neighbour said, "You'll easily find it," and the footsteps changed direction again towards us.

"Is that you, George?" the returning owner said. He appeared, looming out of the mist on the side-path, and said, "Who is this?"

"Someone asking if Mrs Victoria lives here," the neighbour said. "I told him she doesn't."

I did not like the situation. The owner was between me and the gate, and the key that I had put in the back door could be seen gleaming in the light if they looked for it. I had also left the door of the shed partly open. It came to me that if I had been thirty years younger and an energetic man, the fog could have been an advantage. I could have leaped one of the garden fences and made off among the neighbours' gardens. But a fog was no advantage to a man of fifty in a chase on foot by a dog and two men who were ten years younger.

"If Mrs Victoria lived here, my wife would want to know about it, don't you think, George?" the owner said. His sense of humour was as heavy as his shape and his foot-steps.

"I'm sorry," I said. "It's the fog, and all these houses look alike. I'm lost here."

"I never heard of a Mrs Victoria round here," the owner said.

If I had mentioned a name he did know, he would have said I got the address wrong. I felt uncomfortable.

"It's 42 Willoughby," the neighbour said helpfully but sceptically. "He got the Crescent not the Avenue." At the same time the owner seemed to look around at his shed and back door.

"It's as well I didn't want to break in," I said.

The owner said, "Eh?"

I told him, "You left your key in the back door."

"What—?" he said, and pushed past me. He stood looking at the back door. Fortunately, he forgot the shed. He said, "I'll kill that girl."

I began to move a little away from him along the path. I wanted to get a good start for the gate, but I felt at the same time more amazement than fright and an interested surprise. It seemed more surprising than sordid.

"She done it again?" the neighbour said.

"That's the third time." The owner sounded as though he meant what he said and was a man with a heavy hand. "I'll take her pants down."

"For what?" I felt I ought to say. "Children."

"You try the street after the next," the neighbour advised me. They wanted me to go now. "Don't try the next one."

I went a few steps.

47

"I'll take my belt to her," the owner said. His anger seemed exaggerated, as though he were excusing himself. "I'll really belt her." He was a sadistic father.

I suppose I could have owned up that it was I who put the key in the door. I found I did not. I saw I was getting hardened. It was a discovery about myself. I had not expected burglary to harden me. The neighbour said interestedly, "Yes. What is she, eleven now? A girl of her age." I turned and left them.

It was not only that kind of thing. There were other things as well, as I realized. I thought of other houses I had entered. When I was able to enter a house without breaking anything, as I would have done there, with a key or by an open window, I sometimes shifted money around in a house. It was the same principle by which I had disposed of the jewelry that first night. If a wife had money, I would put some of it in a son's drawer or a daughter's handbag. It was expert. Whatever they thought of it, it would be a crime that would not be reported. I had felt desperately guilty about that kind of thing at first, but less so now. It was nothing. It was just that in some subtle way it affected my relations with Margaret.

I went home through the fog thinking about people and looking at the large cars, though most of them were old, parked in the streets of the council estates. Money. A lot of people had it. I thought it would be better not to commit a burglary there that night. It was too late to go off somewhere else, and besides, my nerve was temporarily shaken.

The result was I was early back. Margaret looked at the clock. She had got in the habit of having a hot drink ready.

She said, "You're early."

"Mr Wether has a cold," I said. "He wanted to get to bed early."

She had her own reactions.

"You have wasted a night," she said as she got up. "You have had all that journey for nothing."

"Oh no," I said, defensive. "He'll still pay me."

While she made me my drink, I thought about it.

I had started burglary to keep Margaret happy and in Derrington Drive. At least, that was why I thought I had started it. But was she happy? It did not seem like it that night.

"I wish you did not have to do this secretly, Dalby," she said when she came back.

I did not see why she should keep harping on a "secrecy" that was by then surely nominal. Besides, I wanted to think. If a foggy night did not help burglars, what did help them?

"My dear," I said, sitting down with the drink, "why ever not?"

"It's underhand," she said.

She was capable of better than vague innuendo. I asked her, "In what way?"

"You should tell them. You should tell the Unemployment people. I don't feel comfortable this way."

"You know what would happen."

"I feel you should be honest," she said.

"Yes," I said. "So do I. But then they would deduct what I earned, and there would be no point in my working." I even managed to feel aggrieved about it.

There was some sense in my aggravation. I thought how, if I had been working for a Mr Wether, not only would I have had to report it, but he would have had to stick stamps on my cards, and it would have been so much more expensive and no benefit to either of us. It was not me, it was the system that forced me into dishonest employment; but though I tried, I could not get Margaret to see it in that way, and I felt that I should.

Margaret was sewing, doing our household mending, which she usually did while I was out. While she sewed, she talked, which she could not do on an ordinary night when we were watching television. I was sorry I had come home.

"We can't go on like this, Dalby," she said.

I was a little appalled. There was I, taking dangerous risks

49

to keep us in Derrington Drive, and all she could do was to say that we could not go on in that way.

"Why not?" I said.

"I don't see anyone," she said. "You don't know how difficult it is not to discuss your work with the neighbours."

What she said alarmed me.

"They know that I do it," I said. "What else is there to say but that? For heaven's sake, in any private work, you don't discuss all the details."

"Dalby," she said. "Do you think we could ask Stephanie and David to stay over Christmas?"

I had been married long enough. I mean, I knew the female mind well enough to understand that particular kind of logic, but it was not that at all. It was me that she got at. Why not ask Stephanie, our beloved daughter, and her husband for Christmas? It demanded a Margaret to see why not. It was just that, the moment she suggested it, I saw a spectacle of a family party, sitting down to a turkey in paper hats, and a policeman coming in to arrest me. Yet Margaret did not know that. On the information she had, it was impossible for her to envisage it. Yet at the same time she sensed it.

"No," I said.

"Why not?"

"Margaret," I said, "I am still unemployed." I used a tone of finality. I had money in the tin box in the garage, but I did not tell her that. "We can't afford to entertain them in the style to which they are accustomed, and it is the same reason we did not ask them last Christmas."

"Dalby," she said, reflectively sewing, "we can't go on like this. We can't continue to live in this way."

Stephanie did not even live so far away. They only lived and worked in Southampton; only we never saw them, partly because they had a car while we had none. I wondered. I seemed to have accomplished the reverse of what I had intended. Margaret, for whom I had been prepared to sacrifice myself to keep her in Derrington Drive, was dissatisfied and clearly unhappy. Yet I was gradually becoming aware that I was getting a lot of satisfaction from my life. I did not realize that I was winning, and that Margaret wanting to invite Stephanie was a sign of it. That did not come until too late.

7

On a dark, windy night, on 17 December, I was out in the south-east of the town working around the outskirts. It was the fringe beyond Ramsden Bottom, and when I looked down over the poorer gardens I could see the lights of the factories in the river flats and the railway sidings. It was a bad night and I had only found one house worth entering. If I had had any sense, I would have gone home.

I wandered. I could not see any sense in what I did when it was not worth the money. I was a parasite on society. I did them harm, yet I was becoming interested in people, in the insides of their houses. This was an interest I had not had in the old days.

In the old days, before I had taken to crime myself and seen that there were more ways to live than one, everything had been so dull and ordinary that, apart from my own business and affairs, it had never had any interest. I never looked at houses on a dark wet night, and wondered who lived there, in the bad part of Lockley. Then, I imagined I knew.

I saw a cottage ahead. I was working up a long winding lane. It had led out of town, and it went around at that level. The only reason I was there was that the houses were varied and scattered, but the whole district was too poor, as I could now see. There was no purpose in entering that cottage.

It was dark on the skyline, and it stood in its narrow short garden, with a scrap of wall between hedges. I only looked at it for one reason, because the rain which had started as a drizzle in the night was now blowing up harder on the wind from the south, and if there were some kind of habitation, other things being equal, I would sooner be inside than outside.

Some people are fated probably. Think of the reason I entered Monsen's, the shop with the vacuum cleaner, which was also because of the weather. I am like other people. Fate carefully repeats its lessons, and I don't learn. Even at that, there was not much sense.

It may seem odd that a burglar should make a rush for someone else's cottage merely to get shelter, but it was the kind of thing done by us layabouts and tramps; and in my alternative life, as it might be called, I had rapidly reached that state of accustom. I suppose I would have been satisfied with the lee wall or the shed at the back, but I was surprised, when I went round the side, and tried a back door and it opened. I saw a cottage kitchen that was inviting because across it was a glimpse of firelight.

I was put off. I was no longer the callow kind of burglar who thinks that his main problem is to break into a house, and that everything is solved if he can only effect an entry. I was in shelter of the doorway, and I stopped and I stood there.

Children were the usual reason why a door was left open. I had had experience of that. You start to examine a house where you have found the back door unlocked, and make a creak on the stair, and a little voice calls out, "I can't go to sleep, Daddy". Parents who go out and leave their children, in Lockley, have a phobia. If they lock the children in, the house will burn down in their absence. I got out my torch and started to examine the kitchen. I looked for children's toys in the first place.

There was an easy chair with sagging springs by the fireside. The fire had been backed up, not too early in the evening, and it was evidence that the owner did not intend to come back in a short while. A bare scrubbed table and some hard chairs formed the rest of the furniture. No children's toys,

53

nor children's nor female garments. An ash tray, a packet of St Bruno flake, and a magazine with a nude on the cover. Though the table had no cloth, it held a used knife, fork and plate, and an empty bottle and beer glass. There were more bottles, empty, in the corner. I closed the door behind me and went in at that point.

I followed routine. Like any other criminal, I found it inescapable, and I never felt at ease in a house until I had followed the pattern of actions that I had adopted. After closing the back door, I locked it, and gave hardly another glance to the kitchen. I went through, and down a passage to the front door. That was already bolted. A man's coat hung in the hall. I got the picture then. The cottage was owned by a man who probably lived alone, and when he came back he would head straight for the back door.

I knew there had been a man in that cottage. Or did I? I was safe in the house so long as I remembered that if I heard any sound I must leave by the front. From the evidence, the St Bruno flake and the coat in the hall, I judged the man to be old or middle-aged to old. It was unlikely that he would present any physical danger. I tried the front door and opened it a little to make sure that it opened, then closed it again, and was free to look about me.

It was unlikely that I would find anything to steal in the cottage. I was not sure that I wanted to find anything to steal. As always in that district, there was too much of a difference between my own house in Derrington Drive and the houses I was entering, and I approved of the cottager. A man who lived alone in a cottage, drank his beer and kept himself to himself, came close to an ideal I was forming of a modest life. All the same, I looked in the front room.

It contained a piano, and my torch showed a three-piece suite. There was a dry musty smell, and the narrow beam showed a thick layer of dust. I did not enter the room. It spoke of better times, and perhaps a wife, but it looked as though it had not been used for years. I felt I knew my cottager more, and was even more convinced he was harmless. I thought, and then I decided I might look upstairs.

Old men living alone could not be taken for granted. Every now and again the local newspaper carried an account of one who had died. Everyone had supposed he lived on his pension, but he was found to have a hoard of sovereigns under his bed, or a bank account to the tune of £30,000. I always hoped to find a really large sum of money some time while I was burgling. He was the kind of man who would not have a bank account. I believe I actually hoped that I would not be confronted with an old man's lifetime's savings. As I went up the stairs, listening all the time in case he came back, I noticed that the carpet was threadbare.

I wondered what I was doing in that cottage in fact, and did not approve of myself on that night. The upstairs passage had an angle. There were three rooms, that had probably once been two, but I could see through an open door that the one at the back was a bathroom. I was left to choose between two doors, and I did not think that it mattered which one.

I opened one door, and the first thing that confronted me, on a dressing-table, in the light of my torch, was a woman's handbag. I went forward into the room to get the handbag. I was stupid. It seemed incredible to me a moment later that I had not stopped to realize the existence of the handbag proved I was wrong about all that I had thought and believed I knew about the house.

A light came on almost immediately after I had entered the room. It was an overhead light, but it must have been worked by a switch at the far side of the room. I was still wearing my coat and gloves and my hand was stretched out for the handbag. It was a burglar's nightmare.

A young female voice set up a plaintive wail from a bed. When people discovered a burglar, I was starting to realize, they did not say anything sensible. They seemed to have one-track minds. This one said, "Oh!" and "Who are you?"

I made a mistake. I was too intent on keeping my head and

dealing with situations as they arose, and the prime tendency of a man of my age was to do everything calmly. I turned to her instead of ducking and running away, which would have left her at best with a most confused impression. I spoke steadily to her.

"I beg your pardon," I said. "But I appear to have come in the wrong house."

It was true that I had come into the wrong house, but not in the sense that I meant or that she understood it. It was the wrong house because there, in a room that I had presumed empty, was a young girl. She was aged about sixteen, as I saw when my eyes ceased to be dazzled by the light, in a transparent nightdress leaning over a bed, as she must have done when she switched the light on. Her head was twisted to see me. She was in the house though there had been no trace of her at all downstairs, and she seemed to stay there.

She struggled in the bed rather than sat up in it. I did not understand that at first. I was too dazed by her presence. I was busily absorbing the fact that, no matter what I had seen downstairs, it was visibly a girl's room, untidy and disordered with pictures of male pop-stars on the walls.

"You're not!" she said in a high indignant voice, looking at me from her peculiar angle. "You're a burglar, and you were going for my handbag."

She was the kind of girl who did not hesitate to contradict people, that was clear, and she was more cross and more inclined to assert herself despite her predicament, than she appeared to be at a loss or frightened.

Then I saw a pair of crutches, handy, and leaning in the angle between the wall and the bed-foot.

My reactions were slow, because I was taking it all in: a table by the bed and another plate, knife and fork on it. However, I had the presence of mind to say:

"I am sorry. Do please let me apologize. And I promise I won't touch your handbag."

She stared at me and got herself upright by a kind of scrambling motion on the bed.

"You're a funny kind of burglar," she said, and stared at me as though she did not know what to make, now, of whoever it was who had come in.

It was about that time that I became aware that, young as she was, and crippled as she was, she was very much in a position to give the police my full description.

"That isn't surprising," I said. I wondered whether to smile but decided to treat her seriously. "Because, you see, I'm not one."

"You are," she said.

"I'm not."

"Then who are you?"

"I ..." I said, and tried to think, out of my experience of my own daughter Stephanie, what ought to be convincing '... am a representative of the Lockley and District Providential and Philanthropic Society."

She sat with her mouth open, and I examined her nightdress. The reason it was transparent was that it was threadbare. The whole room was in that state, and I decided that my instinct had been right.

The upper part of her made a pretty, though rather thin and emaciated picture through the nightdress, but I was too preoccupied and could not register much about that at the time.

"You're what?"

"The Lockley and District Providential and Philanthropic."

She stared and almost laughed and said, "The man from the Pru'?" After that, she looked frightened.

"No. The Providential, not the Prudential."

"You've got a cheek," she said.

"Yes," I said.

"Why are you here?" she said. "You were going for my handbag." She was indignant by then as much as frightened.

"I was examining the needs of the district," I said. It

sounded appropriate. "We give comforts in deserving cases."

She thought for a moment. "You've got a cheek," she decided. She disbelieved everything I said, but was unsure.

I said, "Why are you here?"

She put on an expression as though she were talking a foreign language, and said, "I am a polio victim." She was sure of that.

"That sounds deserving."

She looked at me thoughtfully and said, "I want a television." Through her eyelashes, she gave me a quick look.

From the look of the room she wanted, and would benefit by, almost anything. She said, "There's nothing in my handbag."

I looked at items like the carpet on the floor and the pictures on the walls. The carpet was about three feet square and was in the centre of the floor, and where anyone's feet would go if they sat in the chair, there was a hole in the middle. The pictures were pages torn out of girls' magazines. There was a pile of such magazines on the one sagging bookshelf, and they overflowed on to the table and chair and the floor. I wondered how so much interest in pop-art and pop-music could be generated. Somehow, the situation took me back to my childhood. There was a radio on the shelf, an old battered box. They made them to last in that vintage.

I was feeling very bad. I was afraid. I had to silence her somehow.

"A television is a hard thing to get," I said. "I doubt if the Society will give you that before Christmas."

She did not believe in the Society, as I could see by the narrow look she gave me. "I want a television," she said as though that were a test of the truth of my story.

It crossed my mind that I must kill her, yet I talked.

"Why are you here?"

She looked baffled. "I live here."

I looked at the room. "Up here in the dark?" It was as

though I would not need to do anything if she could give a more clear explanation.

She looked frightened again. "I don't like the light." She seemed to sense the change in my thoughts. "I have to live up here because the bathroom is upstairs, but there's nothing to do here."

I remembered how a child's imagination worked best in the dark. At the same time I thought it would probably kill Margaret if I were arrested as a thief, as the burglar of Lockley. Because I did not answer, she said, "You are a burglar, aren't you?"

"Suppose I were a burglar," I said. She looked at me with big eyes. "Would I bring you a television then?"

Her lips parted and she stared. "You might."

"If you did not tell anyone," I said. "But not if you told your father."

I could see her thinking about it. I did not want her to think about it too much, just enough to make it equivocal.

"I am not a burglar," I said. I wondered if it would work. I took out my diary, which served as a notebook, and a pencil. "I represent the Society." I smiled at her. "I want your full name and address." I looked at her and the room. "I can see that you are here."

She said, "Are you really going to get me a television?"

I let her look at me, and I looked at her.

"Yes," I said. "If you don't tell your father."

I knew it could not be done. Nothing would be more likely to make her father ask questions than the appearance of a television in that room.

I could see her thinking. I did not even know if she thought up some lie she could tell him.

"All right," she said. I could see her looking at my notebook and pencil. "Delicia Dobson." She decided to tell me. "42 Langy Lane, in East Lockley."

I noticed the child's way of saying, "in East Lockley."

It was not a good fraud. If I could make her wait a week,

at the end of that time she would realize that she should have told immediately about a man in her room. It would be too difficult to explain. It was the best I could do. At the end of that time she would not tell.

I had a daughter, I knew how their minds worked.

"Delicia," I said, wondering how fate could make it so inappropriate. "That is a nice name."

"My mother gave it to me," she said.

I did not stop to ask her why her mother was absent from that house.

"All right," I said, and closed my notebook and put my pencil away. "You'll get a television, but not before Christmas." I needed to make it as factual as possible. "I may bring it, I may send it."

She looked as though she only half believed me. It was enough. It was a thing she was least likely to tell anyone about, a thing that she only half believed in.

"Goodbye," I said, and stood waiting.

"Goodbye," she said.

I gave her a smile. I pointed to her handbag, that I had not touched, and went out.

I had a reaction on the stairs. I did not have to discover or start to tell myself it was unsatisfactory, for I knew it. I went down using my torch. At the bottom of the stairs I stopped and listened to a faint sound and clatter from her room. In the dark, I wondered if she would come out or start to call out, thinking I was gone; but she did not. I went on to the kitchen. There was a faint glow of firelight.

I stopped there. I was held there by a small pool of light and warmth in the hearth, which showed up the fire-irons. By the table, on the way to the door, I looked at the poker. It was as though it were there telling me to go back and murder her. It crossed my mind that it was wrong. The cleanest way, and the one that would leave least clues, would be to go back and simply strangle her. I wondered why I was thinking of murder. I had carefully chosen a way of crime without violence. I had accepted the risks. What could she say about me? The most she could do would be to help the police to build up my identikit picture.

I can only say that it seemed enough to me, and that the police would be sure to catch me, once they had established my appearance, my clothes and my manner and built up my identikit picture. I went out all the same. I went through the back door into the rain. I made my getaway, and saw no sign of the old man, the father, on the road; and got my bicycle from where I had left it, and rode home.

I was not the same. Pushing the bicycle up the hill to Derrington Drive, I knew I never could be the same. I had been thinking of murder. I did not see where I was going. So far as I was concerned I was still "me", the same person I always had been. How could I be someone else? And why did I think of Delicia Dobson as she was, after I had considered murdering her? I had a glimmering of a feeling. It was still true that I did not know where I was going, except home, but I did have some kind of an apprehension—and that was the right word—that I would have to go somewhere.

8

I HAD BEGUN by theft. I do not know why theft, even small theft, that to most people would have seemed only a minor peccadillo, seemed to me such a large step. It was because I had been so conventional, I presumed. I had not thought about ethics, or my personal morality, or even seriously considered if I had any, no more than do most practical or scientifically-minded or technical people, even of the most academically-minded advanced kinds. Talk to them about ethics or morals, and they take on an expression of suffering. Go on, and they will reveal their impatience. Life is there. They are too busy succeeding in it as it is. It would undo them in some way, it would make all they were doing seem pointless if they were to accept that, by a change of their minds, they could change it.

I was changing my life. I was changing it radically and completely. Even I was becoming aware of the changes. I was no longer even remotely like the person I once was, yet physically and in deeds I had taken only a small step. It was as though I had to catch up with myself, and I did that over Christmas. It began with a small thing.

"Stephanie and David are coming for Christmas," Margaret said, reading a letter the following morning at breakfast.

I could not believe it, and besides, I was thinking.

"I distinctly told you not to ask them." I was angered then, by what I took to be Margaret's conduct. I had not seen the letter she had written to them after we had talked about Christmas.

I was thinking how I could go on with my career of burglary, as I obviously must, though with far greater danger now, if the girl had told her father, and if the police had been furnished with my identikit picture.

"I told you," I said, "not to ask them."

The envelope with their Southampton postmark lay against the marmalade. Margaret was reading their letter. She handed it to me.

Margaret did not defend herself. They were above such things in her family. It would have lessened her dignity. She let me read the letter.

"Surprise, surprise!" Stephanie wrote in her letter. It was in her handwriting that was too like my own. I wondered if all parents' communications from their children looked too like themselves in a false way.

We thought should David make the journey in the car to fetch you to us, and then we had a better idea. You are not to do a thing. You must not even prepare the bedroom. We will bring a turkey and everything. We will entertain you in your own house. You will have to adjust, Mumsie and Dadsie. You will have to put up with a new thing.

Margaret was looking at me and watching me read the letter. "We will need new sheets for the bed in the guest room," she said unemotionally, "and new towels for the bathroom."

It was not she who was to find any way out of the *fait accompli* with which the children had presented us. If anyone was, I was.

"You'll be glad to let them," I said, "have the run of your kitchen?"

"They won't expect that."

"It is what they say."

Impervious to evidence, Margaret said, "They won't expect that."

"We need new curtains for the living-room too," she said.

"They will suspect the worst if they see the state of the old ones."

"You can't have new curtains."

"Mr Wether is giving you extra work for Christmas, and a bonus," she said. "You already said that."

I was being managed.

It was true what the police said about people collecting extra money in their houses at Christmas. I had already been discovering it, during the Christmas-present buying and shopping run-up. In fact I had been doing well on the nights that I had said were Mr Wether's extra work, and I had over £200 in the tin box.

"You can't have new curtains because the neighbours will notice them and see that we're getting more money than we should have." I made a concession. "You can have the new sheets and the towels for the bathroom."

Margaret registered the fact that I could not stop events and could think of no way of averting the children's arrival.

"You are becoming paranoiac over your mild breaches of the law, Dalby," Margaret said. "You are paranoiac." She considered me and the state of my health. "You are suffering from persecution mania." It was a kind of definitive statement.

"Why are they doing this?" I said, proving her point and looking again at the letter. "What do they want? I don't trust them." I was aware I had changed Margaret's thinking.

I gave in through weakness.

It was something I could give Margaret. She could tell the neighbours, with the obscure pride of a lioness with cubs, that the children had bought us our Christmas, and we had had to endure it. It would offer a relief to her unhappiness, somehow. It was something she could say.

I was worried about Margaret. She had stopped telling me I was unethical in not telling the Social Security that I was working part-time. She no longer seemed disturbed that I was cooking my fictional Mr Wether's books. In my relations with the law, she now referred to what she called my "mild breaches". Insensibly, in some way, she had become aware that I had more money than I gave her. It was not only new window curtains that she lived in a state of silently demanding; it was also some new clothes.

I had never understood Margaret in the twenty-five years I had been married to her. It was late to find that out. It had been my presumption that Margaret was worldly and had physical and monetary standards. It had been staring me in the face all the time, though I had not seen it. She was a woman who would starve for an ideal. It had been stupidity on my part to steal in order to give her the Derrington Drive house and good food. Margaret was a Platonist, not an Epicurean. She believed in position and status.

"Margaret," I said, sensing that I had not got things quite right, "what would you like? What would make you supremely happy? If I could, I would give you anything in the world this Christmas?" I had not bought her present.

She thought for a moment. I should have noticed that too. Margaret was very far from a worldly person. She was at home, even more than I was, with propositions that were conditional and abstract.

"You might get yourself made managing director of the new Lee and Lawson's, the big firm," she said thoughtfully. "But it would be enough if you got your job back."

It was another thing I had not been aware of, the cruel streak in Margaret. I had not seen she had one.

"I think you would like that," I said, "if I were just there, and you got no money from it."

It was a peculiar conversation.

"Yes," she said.

Margaret was ordinary. She was orthodox through and through. She wanted the show, not the substance.

"I was thinking of offering you a holiday," I said. "After the children have gone." I set my sights on the distance. "In Taormina."

The effect of my proposition was to make Margaret look as though she were accustomed now to my madness.

"This is something," she said, "that should not be known here in Lockley?"

I understood all too well what she meant, and she knew what I meant.

"Naturally not. After the children have been here, we would say we were off for a few weeks to stay with them."

Margaret looked at me a little oddly.

"Dalby," she said, "how long is it since you started to make a habit of lying?"

It was not simply that Margaret remarked on my new tendency to lie on the least provocation. She would have done that at any time. What was more striking was her lack of indignation. It was something she had noticed, and she had come to accept it.

"It is something we can discuss after Christmas," I said.

"Yes," she said, "it is something we can discuss after Christmas."

I hoped there would be an after Christmas. I intended to continue my burglary, and for all I knew I might be in jail by that time.

I went out, down into the seasonal shopping crowds in Lockley, and looked in at the decorated shop windows, and bought Margaret a hair-dryer; that was something she said she wanted for Christmas. Stephanie and David had said they would bring everything with them, but we were sceptical about the "everything". Margaret bought linen for the house and various items, and I bought adequate drinks for the sideboard. They knew we were unemployed, but we had not mentioned our dire straits to them.

The days to Christmas Eve were uneventful, and they arrived in their car, with a hoot in the street, in the evening.

Stephanie came first into the living-room. "Oh, Mummy and Daddy, how lovely it is to be back!" She had a social air.

She cast a proprietorial air round the room. "Why, everything is just as we left it."

I imagined that what she was looking at, and assessing, was the fact that we had not had to sell anything. Crediting them with normal feelings, I believed that they must have worried and wondered.

Stephanie came back as a young married woman. I did not know what the difference was. A little thicker and clothes that fitted more closely and hair that was more platinum, less like hair more like the genuine metal. It was confidence mostly. Her success in her work was one thing, but it was regular bed with a man, given legal sanction, that had that effect with most females, including my daughter.

David was studiously polite to his wife's parents. Before their arrival, I had shifted the tin box from the spiders' corner to under the floor-boards of the inspection pit in the garage. I hoped, and could see by the clothes he wore now, that he would not want to repair his car while he was with us.

"Darlings!" Stephanie said. "We have so much to do, but let us see how you look first." She put her cheek to her mother.

In fact, as I had anticipated in advance, they did not get the run of the kitchen.

"While I do this," Margaret said on Christmas morning, stuffing the turkey with a certainty that no one could shift, "you get the vacuum and take up the nuts from the carpet."

Stephanie was reduced to discovering we had a new vacuum cleaner, learning again what it was to live with her parents, and why she and Nigel had left home. "I don't like it," she said. The clip of the new machine bit her finger.

No one would suspect, watching Margaret stuff a turkey, that before she had married me she had never done any housework. "I had your father buy me that one specially," she said. "You will know why when you carry one upstairs at my age."

It was something that Margaret and I never discussed,

why we kept up a front to the children. I believe Margaret did it for me in fact. My dignity was hers as she saw it.

"David has something to talk to you about," Stephanie told me that morning.

I had thought that David must have something to talk to me about, but all he said that morning was, "What do you get on investments?"

I did not tell him, "Spiders."

"Seven-and-a-half, eight per cent." I was vague. Fortunately, I had read *The Times* only a few days before.

He was astonished and impressed. "I didn't know anyone dared do that any more, stay in the gilt-edged market."

They were obviously working up to something. "David," Stephanie said, "why don't you ask him?"

But Margaret was calling for slaves from the kitchen.

"No," he told her, "not just now."

Money. I wondered if Stephanie were pregnant. I knew Margaret would think of it. We had Christmas dinner, and I had an odd experience.

No policeman walked up to the door while I was carving the turkey. If the girl with the name had told her father and he had told the police, they were taking a sabbatical on that day. There was a quarrel going on as to which boxes should be used and which paper hats should be worn, out of those we had both provided. It was like something out of Dickens, and I wondered if he had ever done it and written it up: a regular burglar's Christmas. I got David to open the wine, so that we could drink a toast to Nigel; after which we would be receptive, and soporific enough, to subject ourselves to the flow of the Queen's speech.

I had that awkward, incredible, pang-like thought: What are other people's Christmases like? Usually one thought of the starving people of India, but this year it was Delicia Dobson. If there was anyone I did not want to think about, it was her.

I had been thinking about her. I had to. I had to try to

68

calculate, on the basis of the conversation we had had, whether she would have told her father. It had made all the difference in-the world whether I could still move about and be seen in the suburbs. I had decided, No, she would not have told; but to arrive at that conclusion, and change my mind about it several times, I had had to think of her as a person.

In the full, opulent room where we ate in Derrington Drive, I was suddenly remembering, and haunted by, her room. There was no reason for it. It was only a flash, and a kind of nausea, associated with the fact that she lived in that room. If I wanted sentimentality, I thought, I was sure I could find better reasons than that, and soon it was over.

We over-ate. We toasted "absent friends", which included both David's parents and Nigel, and then we toasted them separately. We all felt sorry for the Queen, and agreed she was a wonderful person. David presumably thought it would not be cricket if he made his request at that time.

It was in the evening that Stephanie said, "David, what about now. Haven't you something to say to Father?"

"Oh," he said, "not on Christmas day. We'll talk about it tomorrow sometime."

"No," she said. "Now." I saw what it was to be married to her.

They had already told us that they would be out visiting their Lockley friends all the next day.

I could see Margaret looking to see if Stephanie were pregnant. She was wrong about that. She was not up with the modern mood. Today's parents did not discuss their child before it was born, they discussed it before the conception.

"What is it?" I said. "If you don't tell me now, we will all be bored with the amount of guesswork." I kept calm.

"Oh, it's just that we wondered if you would be interested in a higher rate of interest than you are probably getting," David said.

"Interest?" Margaret looked at Stephanie. "I don't understand him."

I did. I had already got the reason for their visit at Christmas. It gave me a feeling like I had had about Delicia Dobson's room at dinner, only different.

"David thinks he can probably give Daddy better interest on his money than he's getting," Stephanie said as though that fully explained it.

"Actually, we are paying something like twenty per cent," David told me. "Hire purchase and all that. Sixteen on the car."

I wondered on how much. Far more than lay in the tin box in the pit below his car in the garage.

"Stephanie," Margaret said. She tumbled to it. "Are you asking your father for a loan?"

They looked amazed that anyone should say such a thing, in those terms. Who mentioned a loan? They hadn't.

"Oh, Mrs Pearson, Mother," David said. "I don't think what we are thinking of could possibly be said in that way."

"Mother," said Stephanie, "you don't understand finances."

They looked at me as though I might understand it.

"It's not a loan," I said. "You are just asking me to invest in you at a high rate of interest."

"That's it," David said. He put on a mature expression. "A commercial transaction."

"I wish I could," I said. I thought of the piece of string round my tin box. "But my capital is tied up."

They did not come back to it.

Stephanie confined herself to looks. Whenever we were alone, she looked at me.

Margaret started, as soon as we went to bed that night, in a high state of indignation. "A loan," she said. "It was a loan, however they put it. I do not understand them." She felt deeply for me. "And you after your year's unemployment."

By the next day, when we were alone, whilst they were out visiting friends, she was calmer. "I suppose it might have worked," she said. "So long as Stephanie was working and didn't get pregnant."

70

On the third day, the day after Boxing Day, when they had gone and we came back into a house that seemed silent, she said, "I suppose it is a pity. It is a pity, that we can't help our children."

I wondered. They were old enough to think ahead. I did not like to think ill of my children. I did not like them to think they could out-wit me. I still wondered how long they would have kept up the payments, at the high rate of interest.

I could imagine Stephanie looking at me again. "Daddy, you are going to become grandparents. I don't want an abortion." I would ask why an abortion, and she would say that was what it would have to be, if they were to keep up the payments, and it coloured my thinking.

I had a dream when I went to bed that night. It was the kind of dream a burglar is liable to have. It began in the house, where two policemen had come to arrest me, at some time in mid-morning. "There must be some mistake," I remember Margaret saying with dignity. "But I don't understand these things." But we were in the police station at Lockley next, with the swift transition of dreams, and it was apparently midnight.

"We will take you in here to the room," said the policeman who was half a mile high and apparently a sergeant. He did not say, though I knew, that it was where they extracted confessions. I had a feeling I had been there before, with the hard table, the bright light, the bare walls. In my dream, I wondered what happened next, then I saw what they had there. It was Delicia Dobson, whom they had brought in a wheel-chair, though she was still in her nightdress. "That is him," she said sweetly, and proceeded to tell a story about how I had made unmentionable proposals, and then seduced, and then raped her. My denials were made difficult by the fact that, as she went into the details of her story, I was sexually affected.

Margaret was at the police station. It was the way she was dressed perhaps, which included a large hat, that gave her

71

the appearance of being in charge of proceedings. "His name is Dalby Pearson," she repeated at intervals as though it were that which was doubted. "And that is the kind of man he is."

I had to sort myself out. As I have hinted, I already knew that, but it was very far from easy.

I lay awake thinking of my dream. What was right and wrong? I knew what they were. They were what Margaret would have said, in the past, as I saw her in my dream. But, from everything I had read, opinions on that subject always came out in set phrases. They were platitudes, and only of help to the righteous.

9

"Aren't you going out tonight?" Margaret asked.

"Out?"

I am not sure how I made my discovery.

It was at that time, just after Christmas, I am sure. It could not have been as late as mid-January, for that was when we had the big frost. It was the big frost that heralded my new phase of lying, and that was a result, not a cause.

"To Mr Wether's," she said.

It would be comforting, I was thinking even then, if the psychologists were right, and we are not responsible for our actions. I knew it was no use going out that night. There would be no money in any of the houses. With just the two of us in the living-room again, I translated it properly.

"No. He gave me tonight as a holiday. You remember I did extra work before Christmas."

Margaret said sweetly, "Why don't you look at the advertisements instead, and see if you can apply for any jobs in the new year."

I was shocked. For a moment I was without understanding. I know no one will believe this; unless they have criminal experience themselves. It is not laziness that makes one reject the prospect of jobs, it is the discovery that one feels one is unworthy. I shrivelled at the prospect of working. I am trying to tell of a new shift in my cosmos between this and the frost in the new year.

"It's no use applying."

We went to separate rooms in the house and did different things.

I looked out of the window and felt morose about the weather. Margaret could not even do that. When the children had gone, she felt a gap. There was no purpose in her life; she had to invent one. She had no one to manage or react to but me, and nothing to which she could look forward whatsoever. She was suffering some kind of reaction.

It was still afternoon. I heard her searching around the house looking for me. Eventually, she found me. "If you are doing nothing else, Dalby, there is that pipe still to lag in the loft. We don't want a burst again, like the one we had last winter." She had dredged memory until she found something.

It was true that the pipe should be lagged. When we had had the burst, the plumber had repaired but not lagged it.

"I will need to buy lagging before I can do that," I said, "and the shops are not open after Christmas." I turned defence into attack. "Why do you want me to get a job? You have food and heat and the house. You have everything you need except status."

She looked staggered. "Dalby, I don't understand you. I am frightened when you talk in that way."

"Like Stephanie and David," I said.

She said, "What?"

"I decided that during the holiday I had better overhaul the bicycle," I said, and went out, and took refuge in the garage.

It was not very satisfactory in the garage. It was not draughty, for it was solidly constructed, but it was chill and damp and it was abysmally empty. I up-ended the bicycle in the middle of the floor to convince her if she looked in, but I did nothing about it. The garage had two little windows at the back, and I stood looking out of them at the sleet on the lawn. I was someone who had contemplated murder.

I thought. I had broken one moral law, the one about stealing. If you were prepared to break one moral law, was there any reason why you should not break all of them?

I thought of my past life, and it looked somehow distorted. I had been a domesticated animal. Like the people I had robbed, I had been someone whose comings and goings, and whose life, could be forecast. Now I had escaped from my cage. Or I had partly escaped from it. I was standing there, with the gate-bars open, on the edge of the jungle. A sensation of freedom.

What was there out there? What did I want, as a man of fifty? It seemed that never in my life had I asked myself what I wanted before that. Possessions and girls? All right, I said to myself, what do you want? A millionaire's yacht, and a bed full of call-girls? Or a smart office somewhere, and people to obey you, your name on a door plaque?

The arrival and departure of the children had unsettled me just as much as it had Margaret, and for both of us it had come at the wrong time. I might go to prison quite shortly.

I was in a mood in which I wondered if people ever did decide what they wanted. It was as I had thought but not understood, that they just followed the life that was laid out for them, in the place where they were born, whether it be in Lockley or Rome or Mexico. I thought of it with incredulity, as though if people ever stopped to think, what they would want would be to set up a howl, just as I did.

God created the universe, and put man in it, and then said, "Now you think of a purpose." Who was it who said that? Kurt Vonnegut junior.

"Dalby!" Margaret called from the house. "Come for your tea if you want it."

"I can't for the present," I called back. It was getting dark in the garage. It was a short afternoon, and the midwinter gloom was intensifying. "My hands are all dirty."

My hands were not dirty. I had not touched the bicycle. They were in my pockets, keeping warm. I resumed watching through the windows. It lasted a long time.

The joke was that if I had found my freedom, if by theft

75

I had discovered I had always been a domesticated animal, and that there were no barriers, and I could have my freedom, it had come much too late for me. I discovered my trouble, and saw it. I was not grateful for having discovered.

It was a young man who wanted the world, and good food and good wine, to go swimming in the Mediterranean, a yacht full of call-girls. It took a young man with strong wrists and hard nerves to drive fast in a sports car. Life became the more incredible. There were several powerful cars owned by people in the Drive, of the kind that, if I wanted them, I would have to hold up a bank for; except that I did not want them. Only it did not work like that. There was a reality-gap. It was me. I was mentally slipping. Belfont's car, for example. He bought a new Rover 3000 every two years. Could anyone imagine Belfont, taking his wife shopping, using the power of a 3000? In the High Street?

I looked around at my empty garage. A Rover 3000 was a good car, Belfont always said. Built to last. It was so good, and so built to last, that every two years he bought a brand new one.

The cogs were slipping in my mind. It was not just the way it was done now. I no longer believed in the very objectives. A man of fifty should live vicariously. I meant, or I discovered I meant, by giving pleasure to his wife, and second-hand, a little doting, through the lives of his children. My wife, and my children? Aye, there was the rub. That was my discovery, and I discovered it. My lack of a fifty-year-old-man's objective.

I had not seen this before. Margaret had called me to tea, and I imagined her picking at her food. Give pleasure to Margaret? In bed, for example? If only Margaret would take it.

I imagined Stephanie and David. "Here you are, here's your loan." Munificent, no need to tell them I stole it. What would they do? A new house, and a new car, a rise in social status, would they become "a success" in their own way?

Then the discovery, which they would make, that there was another layer just above them. The new "friends" whose income they could not quite equal, and the need to keep up, the rat-race and the categorical imperative to run even harder. It was no gift.

Only three people were successful in the western world, the President of the U.S.A., the Queen, and Paul Getty. Look at it, I told myself with a sense of dismay. All the rest had tragic lives, because they could not get to the top, and they were failures, just like me. Only I was not glad to see it.

I thought, "Tea," and went in to Margaret on that day.

There are depths of despair that I imagine are only normally felt by a manic-depressive, and if this is true then when such people attempt suicide no one should stop them. It is not only that there is no way out and life is a black joke. It really is true at such times, for me, that I am born in a universe that has no aim and no purpose. It is a cheat and all ambition and all hope is no more than a flat way to a grave-yard.

People grow old bravely, and they look at old men and old women, and they learn the truth gradually about cancers and strokes. It is for nothing in the end. The earth and the sun and the stars are all mortal, and when humanity is gone, it will all be as if we had not been, and no one will know it.

If a God, not of love or of vengeance but of malevolence and hate were designing a torture, there would be no better, I imagine, than to endow a creature with health and intelligence and let it know it would lose it, gradually and inexorably, and know too that the reason for its existence would not be found out in its lifetime. There would be no better way of rendering all existence, and every conceivable action quite completely pointless. There is no difference in such a universe between kindness and the use of the whip and the thumbscrew and hot irons.

As though I in particular, already reduced to a thief, had any choice in my actions. It looked that way to me when I went to bed that night, and I came out on the far side.

10

I DO NOT know if it is possible to begin again and live several lives in a lifetime. If it is, then it is ordinary and must be done several times, with no high words and no drama.

"I promised to do an errand for Mr Wether in Lockley tomorrow. If I forget, would you remind me?"

"What kind of errand?" she said.

"It is nothing to do with us, it is just his private business."

In fact, it is impossible to be neutral about anything. It was that tea-time on the Tuesday, and I had roused Margaret's curiosity; she thought I had done it deliberately, and could not bear to be left out.

"You'd better remember it yourself," she said. "Because if you don't, then I won't."

In fact, I had not made my mind up about it, neither that day nor the Wednesday. I could see the pointlessness of action, and of all actions that was, in some way, most pointless.

I was physically attracted. It is easiest to say it in that way. It was the animal drive in a fifty-year-old man. For any psychologist who has got so far as this by chance, I can only point out, of almost all psychological theories, that because a thing cannot be disproved that does not necessarily prove it. On the sober facts as they were, I do not think I would have seen it myself in advance as the most likely of my actions.

"Did you do it?" Margaret said when I came back at lunch-time on the Wednesday.

I wondered if she had been bound to remind me. That could have been forecast. She would not have found out if she had not.

"Do what?"

"Mr Wether's business in Lockley. Whatever it was that you went for."

"No. It's a nuisance. They told me to call back."

"This afternoon?"

"No, the shops will be closed this afternoon. Tomorrow."

It did not do Margaret any harm to think for another day about Mr Wether's business.

When I came back on the Thursday, she did not know it was Mr Wether's business and did not immediately assume so.

It was a very neat television, miniaturized and all-solid-state, in a case of bright plastic. I had looked at one or two older types of box-sets. It had been my original intention to buy Delicia Dobson one of those, a second-hand set at a cheap price. I had thought, what the hell. I had explained it to myself. It had to be something I could carry, and I would have to go there myself, since it would have to be explained to her father.

"Dalby, you haven't bought that?" Margaret said suspiciously, when I brought it into the house, remembering the time I come back with the vacuum cleaner.

I showed her how it worked. I put it on the sideboard and extended its antennae. It was quite a toy for a girl, and it would work on either battery or mains. You could switch it to any of the three wavebands. It was not colour, but as I said, you could not have everything.

"What are you doing with it?"

"It's Mr Wether's. It's been to the shop for repairs. It belongs to his daughter."

I remembered too late that I had said at one time that there was only Mr Wether and his wife, and he did not have any children.

"You told me that Mr Wether did not have a daughter," Margaret said.

I said, "His illegitimate daughter."

"Oh," Margaret said.

I began to see it was an advantage if Mr Wether's character were developed. I was not exploiting him enough. But for the moment it was sufficient that Margaret put on an expression as though she had always suspected that Mr Wether was the kind of man who would have tangled matrimonial affairs and illegitimate daughters. I was absorbed in the project before me.

I doubted very much whether the crippled girl, when she had asked for a television, had thought how she was going to explain its sudden appearance to her father. I would have to be convincing. It crossed my mind that before Christmas I had been in a state of terror lest her father should know. Now I was looking forward to seeing Delicia Dobson again. The amount I had spent on the television was an indication of my peculiar excitement.

I had several reversals of feeling before the Friday night that I went there. At one time on the Friday morning, the whole episode seemed to me to be thoroughly mad. I would have to appear. If I could not leave the explanations to the girl herself, I would have to talk to the father. How did I know that they had not already told the police? For all I knew the police might be keeping a watch on the house in case I returned. I wondered what I could do with the television I had landed myself with, and if I could sell it. I was not clear what my aim was.

In the afternoon it seemed equally obvious to me that no harm could be done to me by poor people on the far side of Lockley. All I wondered about then was whether I could catch the father out and have a talk with the girl before I saw him. I was a messenger from the Gods. I was bringing television into their lives. It must confirm that I was a philanthropist, and they could not possibly suspect me.

I could have wished there were not such a cold north wind blowing that night, but at least it was not raining.

"How are you going to carry that?" Margaret said when I

picked up the television to go out. I felt I was offering my fate to chance as though I were playing some game of Russian Roulette. At the same time I had an elevation of feeling as though I were going off for a secret tryst with a girl-friend. I told her I would strap it to the back of the bicycle.

I rode down the hill to the town and through the centre of Lockley. All the way as I was going in the cold windy night the errand on which I was engaged seemed more stupid. My feeling about the insanity of what I was doing reached its peak as I went up the mean streets at the back of the town, behind Ramsden Bottom, to the lane and the cottage. To get out of Lockley on that side too I had to go up a hill and push the bicycle past street lamps and rows of back-to-back houses. When I came in sight of the cottage, I saw that the girl's bedroom light was on. When I stood with the bicycle in the lane outside the garden, I could see a faint reflection on the broken wall and the shed at the back. There was also a light in the kitchen.

I wondered whether to dump the television in the nearest ditch and ride off. At least I could see no sign of the police, who I imagined might be watching from parked cars. The wind blew bleakly down the lane, and I knew that quite soon I would be freezing. Why was I there? Love or sex? The girl was a cripple. In any of the pubs in that district, I could have found a girl-friend. In the lane in the cold wind, I thought of morality and ethics. I tried to think of a thought I had had about acting on my own moral system, but it seemed strangely distant. Moral systems were not that easy.

I was there. I had a dim memory, from what seemed a century ago, of wartime in Italy. I dumped the bicycle in the hedge. I took the television and marched up to the front door.

I rang the bell and it did not work, and I had to knock, standing there in the shadows.

"Hello," he said when he came to the front door.

He was a Lockley working-class man, in carpet slippers and baggy trousers and braces. Delicia Dobson's father.

82

"Good evening," I said. "Mr Dobson, I believe? I represent the Lockley and District Providential and Philanthropic Society. I am making enquiries—"

"We don't want any," he said, and stood holding the door with the light partly on him. He was like that.

I did not get his drift for a moment. I was too busy seeing he showed no signs of a wish to arrest me.

"If it's insurance, we don't have any," he said. He was as stolid as only a Lockley working-class man could be. "We don't make contributions." He was a slack-looking fat man.

I had to act. He showed no signs of haste, but he was going to close the door at any moment. He was the girl's father.

I held up the television where he could see it in the light. "Mr Dobson," I said, "I have brought this for your daughter."

"We can't afford it," he said.

"It's a television, and it's free."

"Ah," he said, grudgingly opening the door a little more, "but who's to pay for the licence?"

I had a dream-like feeling when I first went into the Dobson house. I had considered all kinds of receptions before I got there. The one thing I had not considered was who was to pay for the licence. I saw life existed.

We went through into the kitchen where I had at one time stood and looked at the fire-irons. Life was real. It was something, it seemed to me, of which I had not been adequately or fully aware. It was real for other people. He sat in his easy chair by the fire. He showed no sign of good manners. He left it to me to seat myself on a hard chair by the table.

"They wanted to give us one once before," he said.

"Who did?"

"The people who give televisions to the sick." He was comfortable by his fireside, a morbidly self-satisfied fat man. He began to fill his pipe. What had I expected Delicia Dobson's father to be like? He said, "They wanted us to pay for the licence." He spilled his tobacco.

I wondered whether I could pay for the licence and send him out to get change while I talked to the girl. I had come prepared. I took out my diary. It was the same one in which I had written down Delicia's name and address. I had torn out that page in case the police should discover it on me, but it served as a notebook.

"We'll discuss that, Mr Dobson. The first thing I want is a few details of the family for our records."

"What particularly do you want?" He looked away with an evasive sly look. I was a Derrington Drive man.

"Her mother."

Looking firmly away, he told me, "She left me."

I wrote it down. "She left me."

"Why?" I said.

"It wasn't good enough."

I wrote that down too, then asked him, "What wasn't good enough?"

"Looking after me and our daughter."

I wondered what it would be like, doing that permanently, if I were a genuine social worker.

"They get good wages in Coventry."

"Why Coventry?"

"Because that's where they get good wages."

"Mr Dobson."

"Yerse?"

"What shall we do about the licence?"

"Is that a television?" he said, looking at the set I had put on the table.

I switched it on and showed him that it worked.

"It isn't a proper television. It's only a small one."

"The licence costs the same anyway." Defensively, I said, "I thought that she'd like it."

"Oh, yerse, she'd probably like it."

While I was writing that down, he said, "You was the one who came here before Christmas?"

I looked up at him, "I think she thought I was a burglar."

84

"Yerse," he said. "She thought you were a burglar."

I looked at him closely. "You didn't?"

"I didn't see a burglar coming in to take nothing from us."

I nodded. A little dryly, like someone who owned a house on Derrington Drive, I said, "You haven't a lot here."

He looked back at me. "She swore you did nothing with her."

"Mr Dobson," I said, "I could do better than your daughter."

He looked at me and said, "Yerse. I suppose you could."

"I am thinking of paying for a television licence for you out of my own pocket," I said.

I could see by the look of him that he was for the most part unemployed, and he said, "There's one thing. She can't have a television unless the licence is paid for."

He was the kind of man who was the despair of those who had tried to set up the Welfare State in my generation.

I supposed I was there for philanthropy. I was trying it out. I had no rules to hold me, but I had not the ego nor the self-deception to make myself rich for no reason. I was trying it out. I was seeing what it was like, to give pleasure gratuitously, to some other person. I felt in my pocket, and I extracted my wallet, and I took out two five-pounds.

"I need change to give you money for a licence, for seven pounds. Have you got it?"

He looked at the money greedily and said, "I've had no money since Christmas."

"You can go out to a pub and get it," I said. "I'll wait. But I'll buy you only one drink there."

"You got a cheek," he said.

"Christ, I'm giving you this. I don't need to give you a damn thing."

"You want me to leave you with her," he said. "How do I know what you're after?"

"If I wanted to go to bed with a girl, Mr Dobson, I wouldn't choose one who's paralysed, who can't walk."

85

He began to put his workman's boots on. He understood something. He knew he would have to do it eventually. It was not even what you said. It was a tone of voice and an attitude. I had wondered about it sometimes, how you make them do things, and remembered my Lee and Lawson experience.

"You stay down here while I'm gone," he said.

"I shall go up to the bedroom and have the pleasure of giving her a television," I said. "That's all I get out of it."

It was true, too. I thought of those men, Frank Lofthouse, Fred Ginmer and Tom Walsman, the only old men I knew who had stupid young girls apart from their wives. Everyone said it was sex and that they were dirty old men. They did not deny it, and Frank Lofthouse even confirmed it. But I wondered. They all had wives who only wanted the impossible, like my wife. We all met sometimes in the bar, and when one of them produced a package from his pocket and gave it to his girl, her young face would light up. They had all been throwing themselves away on worthless girls, I thought as I watched Dobson go out.

"I'll be back," he said.

"Don't spend it all," I said. "You've got a television licence to buy, and I will want nearly three pounds." I knew that he would not spend the money on a television licence just as well as he did.

I picked up the television and took it upstairs. I wondered if he cared what I did with Delicia. I thought probably he did. He would want to blackmail me if he could get a hold on me somehow. "It's me," I said, and knocked on her bedroom door and went in.

She was sitting up in bed, and she put her arm over her breasts and looked more startled in that way that time.

"Oh, it's you." She did not seem particularly surprised it was me.

I held the television in my hand in the doorway and switched the vision on, on battery, knowing she would never have seen a television come on instantly and work while held in the hand just in that way. "I've come to tell you you can't have your television," I said, "because you told your father about me."

I saw her look, and see me and the vision, and her eyes partly light up. She did not believe I could have brought it only to take away again, despite my serious face. She took her hands away from her breasts, and started a tentative smile, and said, "Why, it is you!"

Could I be so bad, just to show her the set and take it away? I tried to tell myself I could. I had once thought of murdering her, and that had been real for a moment.

Her eyes seemed to watch me and her expression to hang. Then her smile increased, and she became more excited. She put her hands out, and seemed to start to move up and down in bed, and said, "You are going to give it to me, aren't you?"

It was damnable. The girl was a cripple, the room was sordid, and she was no very great beauty. Just young, and normally, as I had seen, a little bitter, and yet rash, and thoroughly irresponsible, and capable of making up her own mind about faces.

"You're a bad, bad girl," I said, putting it on her table where she could only just reach it. "And you don't in the least deserve it."

She had her hand on it. She had met televisions before, and soon found the vision and the volume. She stopped being a young child and gave me a sixteen-year-old look, and said, "Are you really a burglar?"

I found myself the chair, and pulled it to the bed. I looked at her expression and the curves, and the awkwardness of her body, reflected in her movements and the way she sat.

Who was I kidding, telling myself that I had come back, as a random experiment, to bring some pleasure into the life of Delicia Dobson? It was I who got the pleasure. I was a *voyeur* of the girl. I was a parent to the child, a sadist to

87

the vulnerability, a masochist to the fact that she saw me as an old man, and a parasite to the life that seemed to bubble out of the bed from all her parts and pieces.

I was grinning at her because it was a matter of such serious importance, and at the same time a joke, whether I were a burglar. "No!"

"Then why did you tell me not to tell my father?"

"I was testing you. I was trying you out, and you failed."

"Then why have you brought me the television?"

"I told you. I have just brought it to show you, and then I am going to take it away."

"I don't believe you."

What did I expect? I had pulled up the chair by then, and I was sitting on it, very close to the bed. What were we going to do? We were going to talk a great deal of nonsense. She had to pull herself half out of the bed to reach the television, and she behaved like a child; but at the same time, while the tiny speaker yelled out a song and she tried to control it, she looked sideways to see how I watched her.

It was not the kind of conversation that would be capable of analysis or that would bear any reporting.

"Oh," she said. "I think you are a bad man."

How does one record a statement like that, with all its concomitant of expressions and glances? For example, just why should she say it?

"You're terrible."

"Why?"

"Here I am, risking prison to bring you a—"

"Oh!"

So we talked about kissing.

What else was there to talk about? After all, the obviousness was the point, the logic, that I had to know what I would get for the set if I left it.

Dobson took his time at the pub. "I can't kiss you," she said.

"Why not?"

Her body, with a life of its own, was inviting. Either her eyes were solemn while her lips had a curve, or her eyes danced while it was her face that was caustic. Dobson was back in time to save the honour of his daughter.

"How do I know what you would do? I don't know you."

I wondered. If I tried hard?

When Dobson came in, he took a look. It must have been her colour or her attitude, for I was sitting in the chair on the far side of the room. He said, "Put your bed-jacket on, girl!"

11

THE NIGHT WAS dark when I went out. I felt partly sane.

It was an experiment, and I presumed I had to think if it had been successful. I did not know when I went out to return to my bicycle. I would find out.

Successful in what? In passing the time? In arousing lechery in the mind (and at times the body) of a man who was maudlin? Any other girl would do, I told myself. I could see that. I stumbled in the garden. I did not see.

Or would they? Poor Margaret, I thought, as I communed with the night stars. I got on the bicycle rapidly. It was too cold for communion.

Then I took my time about going home. This was part of the experience of being fifty years old, even riding a bicycle carefully down a hill and round the dark corners of a lane. Between two females. Though it was a cold windy night and he was out in it, no cautious man would rush back to the first one. I noticed symptoms in myself.

The lights of Lockley had a soulful appearance. There was a mystery about houses and dark fields and hedgerows. I thought of the people in the town, and the isolation of their lives, and the bedrooms, and the small children sleeping. Like taking my temperature, I decided the symptoms were mild ones. They had better be, I thought.

It was like capturing some spiritual part of myself, that had a tendency to fly out. It was in a state of deprivation, this spiritual arm, and I had to control it, as though against some centrifugal force or a magnetic attraction. It was not a case of having a sentimental attachment but of noticing a tendency towards an attachment.

I went down through the town streets wishing there was somewhere I could stop and think. A pub perhaps? I heard singing, saw lights at a window, and heard the sounds of a crowd as I passed one. I stopped somewhere else, and my feelings betrayed me.

"£2,224 ex-works," said a red-lettered card. It was on the other side of plate glass, and I had stopped, of all places, with one foot on the kerb, outside a car-showrooms on the corner of the High Street.

I would not say, or it did not appear to be at the time, that it was a revolution in my cosmos. A nice gleaming car, and a footnote to the sign, "Automatic De-Luxe, £315.35 Extra".

One thing I had done while with Delicia had been to confirm that she lived upstairs because of the bathroom. Their bathroom was upstairs, and she could not climb the stairs. Or she could, but it was a great deal of trouble, needing help, and she was liable to fall when she came down. Which was a pity, for she had a wheel-chair in the shed at the back of the house, provided by someone; and if she could live in the room downstairs, with a bathroom adjacent, and had a way to get the wheel-chair in and out of the front door, her life would approximate, almost nearly, to that of a cripple who was cared for.

I stood on the corner, or rather sat on the bicycle, pausing for a moment in my journey across town, looking in at the lighted showroom, between the side street I was going to take and the lights along the High Street.

I had restrained myself, while I was in the house with Delicia, from trying to get her out of bed to see how she could walk, or dealing with her practical problems. But I gave a thought to them now. I thought of her trapped in her bedroom, and I wondered how often Dobson gave her assistance; or, more than that, the positive urging and determination, to get out, to meet people and to encounter the world and the fresh air and the sunlight. Why had I not seen, when I was there, that that was her real problem? I was the more culpable in that it was one of which I had heard, as an indictment of local authorities and the social services, that they provided wheel-chairs and sometimes invalid carriages, but made no provision to see that those concerned could live downstairs or could get downstairs to use them.

I had been in the house, but I had missed the main point, and now the sign had caught my eye, "£2,224 ex-works, Automatic De-Luxe, £315.35 Extra". It was in my head before I knew it, as I looked at the gleam of the car and the potted palms in the showroom, that I, if I had not been made redundant, would probably have bought that car. And that to transform Delicia Dobson's whole life what was needed was not the cost of the car, but the "£315.35 Extra".

They were thoughts on a mid-winter night; what kind of a world did we live in? I was visualizing someone in the showroom, myself or perhaps Belfont, saying Yes to the little lever on the steering column and the shade extra comfort. It was what? Instinct or guilt? I turned, and looked over my shoulder, and saw a policeman up the High Street.

They stood in doorways there, watching the street where some of the shop windows were lighted, but he had moved out, solid in his uniform and no doubt bored, and was looking straight at me. I was "loitering with intent". With what intent? He must have seen the way I looked over my shoulder at him, as guilty as though I had the intention of putting a brick through the plate glass.

How did he guess that that was how I felt? I had not in my life felt that way before, and I had often looked in that window. My mind, when I had been a car-owner, had not made the most obvious connections between the waste and the pity. I looked backwards and sideways up the street, and he began to walk down towards me.

I waited until he had got half-way down towards me, then

pushed off from the kerb, and left him, and went off down the side street.

I felt fear after I had done that. I had made myself conspicuous, I had drawn his attention. It loomed in my mind. For all I knew, he would make a note, pass in a "suspicious character" report. Delicia and Dobson had not reported me to the police, but it was through them I wondered how long my burglaries could be continued, if, as seemed likely from the move of the policeman, they were looking out for a cyclist in Lockley.

As I pushed the bicycle up the hill going home, I thought of Dobson's return from the pub, and the way I had left him. I had told him I would be back, and he had asked what for. I had pointed to the television. "To see that you haven't taken this out and sold it." I had told Delicia I would bring her something else, and I thought of my depleted money in the tin box in the garage.

I was not sure if I was shaping events. I had more of the sensation of sinking deeper into a pit. It was more that events were shaping me, to the start of a new life.

12

I SAY "I think" and "I presume" that this and that happened, and I know very well that this is not the way to interest any readers. I do not think it can be helped. I know too well how easy it is to tell, and even to see in the mind and remember, not the truth, but a version of something.

If anything of importance has happened, especially between husband and wife, in the way of a row or a scene, then almost as soon as it has happened, as we all know, we start to go over it and improve it. Very soon what we remember is not the truth. It is the mind's reconstruction.

I had written this version of what happened when Margaret discovered that Mr Wether did not exist, not three or four times, but a dozen, and each time improved it.

Each time it got "better" from a reader's point of view, it got worse. I have gone back to my first notes.

The first note I have says, "Margaret looking out of the window." I know, from the way I have written that, as a single line on its own, that I intended not only to describe the scene, of Margaret looking out at the snowy waste on the lawn, but to use it in some way to describe our relations since Christmas. And in some of my versions it was this I attempted.

The fact is that I do not remember what our relations were after Christmas. I would have to invent them. And in inventing them, even though I did it with the utmost truth of which I was capable, I would destroy the point of the story.

I did not notice what my relations with Margaret were after Christmas. This is the point. I was thinking about Delicia Dobson, and money, and my relations with the world and society, and similar obsessed things. Margaret was too familiar. She was nearer to me than anyone else, and yet her reactions seemed too easy to forecast, like her statement "We can't live in this way." It is too easy to say that I should not have let her become what I did let her become, just a figure in the background.

When Margaret drew my attention to the way the snow was staying, what I remember about it is not Margaret looking out of the window with her hand on the curtain, but the thought I had that I would not be able to go to visit Delicia that night. I remember that and my own view of the snow, and my realization, as I looked out from the warmth of the house at the Drive, that I could not use the bicycle on it at all, not for burglary either, because it was frozen and rutted.

Snow followed by a frost like that was something that happened in Lockley about once every two years, and what was noticeable from our room when it did was the silence. I remember listening, and deriving from the silence through the window that traffic was stopped on the main road, so it had settled, and I felt something of a young lover's or infatuated old man's disappointment about it, because I would not be able to go see Delicia for the third time since Christmas, even by bus.

Margaret said something like, "What are you going to do? You won't be able to go to Mr Wether's," and I said, without giving more than half my mind to it, "I'll go out and 'phone him."

I was certainly not aware that I had put it into Margaret's mind that it was possible to 'phone Mr Wether. I went out in fact, since I had said it, and pretended to go to the 'phone on the corner. I looked at the snow in the drives of the houses, and thought how a burglar would be a fool, even though it was frozen, to risk footprints, and came back to be confined with Margaret for three days.

Of those three days, what I remember chiefly is Margaret's nagging annoyance because I had still not lagged the pipe in our loft, with the result that the bathroom cold taps were frozen, and she could not take a bath. When the thaw came suddenly, and the snow slid off the roofs of the houses at midday under winter sunlight and a wind from the south, I forgot that entirely, and announced, despite Margaret's reasonable objections about what the roads would be like to Conlea, that I must go to Mr Wether that night. I had been brooding. I had thought that, what with one of my weekly "Mr Wether" nights now occupied with visits to Delicia, and the snow, and the prospect of lighter nights soon now the year had turned, I was going to have difficulty keeping up enough income from my burglary, far less being able to do something for Delicia. I had determined to go out again as soon as I was possibly able.

I did not realize what I had done by this combination of circumstances until I got back. Even then, riding up the Drive and being wary of slush on the road, when I saw the lights in the house, I only thought that the pipe had thawed and that Margaret had been able to take her bath—which was adequate explanation for the lights in the hall and the landing and bathroom.

It was only when I put the bicycle away in the garage and came in by the back door, that I heard voices and noticed that we also had lights in the living-room and kitchen. As I came through the kitchen, I noticed a line of drips on the floor between the sink and the hall. It was from the hall that the voices came. A male voice mumbled something like "I think I can hear him", and I recognized McFarlane from next door.

Margaret called out, "Dalby!"

I was extremely slow on the uptake.

Margaret and McFarlane were in the hall. They had a

bucket and a mop and pail and a large plastic sponge. They were trying to soak up water that was running out of the stair-carpet. From the upstairs landing, the light shone down on a scene of devastation I had not seen—where the water must have come from.

We all know these things happen. Even if they have happened before, it never seems to us that they can be happening now, and again. It was just a pipe-burst, the kind of thing that keeps plumbers in business. It was still there, with its revelation that things that had been thought permanent, and valuable, and the established fabric of our lives, were not so. Margaret stared at me as I came in, and I believed I knew what she was thinking.

She had warned me about that pipe. She had warned me more than once. I had not merely done nothing about it, I who was unemployed and had done nothing for three days, but when the thaw came, when the crisis happened, I had gone out and left her. That was what I thought she was thinking.

I was dressed in the heavy outdoor clothes I used for cycling, the same clothes I used for burglary as well as for visiting Delicia; I was self-conscious that McFarlane should see me like that, and be present at a confrontation between Margaret and me that should have been private, domestic.

I am making excuses. I am excusing myself for not seeing what had happened, what must have, despite my sensations.

"What has happened?" I asked it, coming in and blinking in the light. But I believed that I knew what had happened.

I could see the way they looked at me, the late-comer to the scene: McFarlane blank-faced, a little strange, both silent, waiting for me to see and for things to speak for themselves; and Margaret strained and still, with what I thought was her particularly dangerous stillness, as well as silent.

McFarlane looked at Margaret. I stood by the stairs and they were nearer the front door. It struck me they were behaving a little oddly, that it was McFarlane who spoke,

97

his elderly face twisting and becoming a grimace.

"Margaret called me ... I turned off the stop-cock." He made a gesture inviting me to look, to see why he had done that. "It was nothing." He became agitated, replying as though I had thanked him, though I had not. "What anyone would do ... you don't need ... the 'phone calls." He seemed disconnected.

Margaret was staring at me not as though she were looking at me, which would have meant communication, but as though she saw me, as something new, as something to be looked at, from head to foot without moving her eyes or her face, as a whole man, an object.

I wondered. The bathroom ceiling down? Or perhaps in the bedroom? Was it that bad? It was all dreadfully slow. I even turned and looked up the stairs, until I registered, and I started to notice, to realize I had heard the one thing. I turned back more quickly, and looked at McFarlane.

"The 'phone calls?" I suddenly felt that.

I had an abrupt and sinking sensation.

"A plumber ... Margaret thought if she could get you ..." McFarlane moved his hands. He had a mop in one of them. It was as though he had to make explanations. "The 'phone ... I mean you don't need ... they were mostly to directory inquiries, local, the builders in Conlea ..." His eyes looked off sideways.

I understood it in layers, like stages.

Margaret. I knew why she looked as she did. She knew there was no Mr Wether. For months I had deceived her.

But the 'phone. She had used the 'phone in the McFarlanes, and they had assisted. That meant also that they knew. They knew that I had deceived them and Margaret. By tomorrow all Derrington Drive would know, they would tell it.

I thought, the police ... I suddenly saw the whole thing.

A man in my position, living as I was, was vulnerable. For a while, everything went well, and then suddenly it happened. It was thinking that which occupied my mind, and the realization that it had happened. I could not start to make explanations. It was catastrophe from a blue sky.

The drama played inside me. I seemed to have a drumming in my head, the knowledge that it was important, that it was quite out of scale with burst pipes. I did not know what to do. When I came to the crisis, I did not know what to do. I looked at Margaret, and she stared at me for a moment, then she looked at McFarlane. I got that. I saw what I must do.

I took my orders from her. I blinked, then I knew what she meant when she looked at McFarlane. I stirred and went to him.

"Yes," I said. "I understand. You have been a big help." I could see myself smiling and acting. "But we can't keep you now. I'm back, as you see." I reached past him and opened the front door.

He stood surprised. He genuinely looked as though he expected to stay there. "If I can help ... you'll want to see ..." He had his priorities all wrong. "In the bathroom ..."

"Yes," I said. "But I'll see to it. Look. You have your feet wet ..." I put my hand on his arm. I pushed him quite gently. He looked surprised again, injured.

Out of nowhere in my mind came the thought that I ought to explain. Tell him that Mr Wether had changed his 'phone number? But they had tried the exchange. "I suppose you tried Mr Wether." I had him on the doorstep. "You should have tried, I mean, in the firm's name ..." It would not do. Mary McFarlane would expect details from Margaret, about which firm it was. I just imagined, against all reason, that it would hold him until morning, though I had heard they had tried all the builders. But I stood smiling, still acting while he backed out, then I closed the door on him. I knew it was fatal.

With the door closed, Margaret and I looked at one another in the wet hall. Now it was starting.

I thought, this was the worst. Getting caught, being arrested and taken to court would be an anti-climax after this.

Margaret's voice was solid and blank. It was maybe the damp and the water in the hall that supplied the image. She was the captain on the bridge. She was in the Admiralty. She announced some naval disaster. She stood rock-solid in the wet hall, so very much there with her grey hair and the damp on the hem of her house dress.

She was perpetual, my life and my marriage.

"Dalby," she said. "Dalby. They think you have another woman, that that's where you go in the evenings."

It was true. How could it be true? It was Delicia Dobson I had come from, that night.

Disaster.

Her disaster.

13

I was to be occupied with Margaret for a long time. All other business took second place in my attention. It was just trying to keep things as they were.

"Dalby, just why have you deceived me?"

We repeated things. We said the same things in different ways. We went round and round. We made the same discoveries twice.

I turned to go into the living-room, and then realized I could not simply not answer that one. I turned back to her.

"Because I had to."

"Have you thought of the humiliation," her eyes fixed me, "of having them there when I found out?"

What could I say? "I warned you."

She stared. After a moment: "I don't remember."

"I told you not to talk about my work, to any of the neighbours. You told him Mr Wether's name."

"Dalby, don't shout."

"I have reason to shout. Do you know what you have done?"

She stared at my unreason. "... because they think you have another woman to go to?"

I was staggered again. That she should use it. That she should use the McFarlanes against me. I would have laughed if I could. I made a gesture to the door. "Him?"

"Not him. Her. But he will by morning." Margaret looked at me bleakly. She was terribly actual.

I had started to shout, and it had been strangled. To shout and to bluster was the thing I most wanted.

I had not lived with Margaret for a quarter century without learning. We were no different from any other married couple after that length of time. We each knew the other's armaments and which thrusts were most deadly.

I said, "If you think that . . . !" I hoped that I knew her.

It crossed my mind again after I had said it, not before, that I had been with Delicia Dobson that evening.

"I did not say I thought it, Dalby." She looked at me. "I don't think you have a woman who will pay you."

She reduced me to the feeling I was crawling on the floor. Had she been in the wrong, it would have been her. Between us, it was the way that it worked out.

She looked at the stairs. "You have not yet seen it," she said. She considered the devastation for a moment. She looked as though she were going to cry. She did not cry. That would not have been Margaret. She went into the living-room before me, her tallness, her straight back.

"You had better tell me now. It is only *things* that are spoiled upstairs. Then you can go round and make a clean breast to them in the morning."

I was following her into the room. I said, "I don't intend to tell them any more than I have done."

She swung round and stared. "Dalby! Not even you could let them go on thinking—"

"I must."

"Dalby, for God's sake! The story that you deceive me will be all round the district." I think she was frightened.

"I can't help it, dear. Believe me, it was not my intention."

"Then what is . . . what was your intention?"

We got to our places by the fire. We stood, we did not sit for the first hour. About midnight, I had thought enough.

"His name is not Mr Wether. 'You don't tell your wife about this,' is the first thing he told me. It is more illegal, dear. It could mean prison, not a fine. It's a little worse than I told you."

It went on, and on, and on.

"Dalby, what is it you are mixed up in?"

We went to bed about three or four. I wondered what marriage was. I remember Margaret hammering, trying to find out what it was that I did.

"He doesn't pay you enough," she repeated, "if it is so illegal."

When we went to bed, we were too tired to sleep. All it meant when we put the light out was the kind of armistice in which we had arranged to stop speaking. I thought of her and Delicia until something like dawn. What happened was that it became clear to me that she was right in her statement. Nothing could be payment enough for that night.

I tried to see it. People thought that crime was a voluntary business, and that people did it for the pleasures it brought, which they should be punished for enjoying; while the sentences handed out for small crimes, for house-breaking and stealing even small sums of money, were right out of proportion. Pleasures—!

I could not see it. I lay tossing and turning. People's reactions were quite out of scale with my actions. Or I was out of scale. As I veered towards sleep, I thought of some wild things I could do; my mind went off into wild, disconnected projects, not seeing that the circumstances I allowed for one would not apply to those I allowed for the next one. It was not exactly violence. I had not quite come to that. To sleep at all, I had to still think I could somehow escape it. It was the small boy's and the desperate old man's thought that I slept on. It was the salvation of the weak man, and for all I know, of women.

It was a trigger for sleep. As I slept, I was thinking, I'll show them. But Margaret, in the next bed, was a vast unsolved question.

14

AWAKENING.

It was the same world, and the world long-established by
the way we live our lives, and the one on which I or anyone
else is fitted to report, the one to which I awoke in the
morning.

We know now, in our generation, some of the mechanisms
that rule us. Sleep restores the connections in the mind. I
had heard somewhere, almost certainly in some television
programme, since that is the way we live, that someone has
proved it. I did not make enough connections.

I slept late. Margaret was up. I could start with my thinking. She had pulled the curtains. I could look at the daylight.

Did my neighbours, not only the McFarlanes but the other
people in Derrington Drive, believe that my movements were
explained by the fact that I had a mistress? It was one thing
I wondered. It was impossible to know. No one knows what his
neighbours think, or what they say about him, behind closed
doors. I wondered then whether the McFarlanes had seized
a chance to set up a situation in which they would find out,
and see Margaret find out, that there was no Mr Wether.

It was possible that I was innocent. I was one of those
people who had always lived in the belief that by and large
people did not act with merely gratuitous malevolence. Perhaps they did. Or it was more likely that life worked slowly,
and it could still be out-witted, since what happened happened only slowly, by a combination of chances.

I had got hope again, by the time that I came down. What
had happened had happened, but it was not an impossible

situation when I came to explore it. I started to look for ways out. I was more like I had been on the morning of the day before. I went on in that way.

I knew there would be consequences. In the language of crime, my "cover story" had been "blown". It was ironic that, in destroying the lies I had told, Derrington Drive had invented a new story for me, even better.

As I came into the kitchen I knew Margaret could not be expected to be happy with the story that I had a mistress. It would make life impossible for her. It would have taken a saint to agree to play the part of a deceived wife in Derrington Drive, and she was no saint. It had been bad enough before that.

She looked up from the stove. She had heard me moving and was making me a breakfast.

"You must go round to the McFarlanes."

I began to see how we would live as I sat down. It was not only that morning. It would go on for the next days.

"To tell them what?"

"To tell them what you have told me, that you are not working for Mr Wether, but for someone else, and it's secret."

Had I said that? It became clear even to my reluctant mind that I had said too much the previous night, and I was getting in deeper.

I worked on it. By lunch-time I had prevailed on Margaret to see that if I told them that it would be useless, because they would not believe me.

She did not like it.

"If they won't believe you, Dalby, why should I believe you?"

I did not know. I looked at her. Why should she believe? And why had I told the story? I had to say something.

"Because you see the money I bring back from work. You take it and use it."

It was astonishing what was credible, what had to be believed, when the facts were as stated. It was less flattering, and more true, that Margaret only believed what I said because there had to be something. She could not credit that I had a mistress who paid me.

I was almost tempted to say, "Why don't you believe that?" and "How do you know?" I retained just enough common sense, and in truth was too frightened by the way things were developing, to say such things. It was Margaret who gave herself the liberty of a free tongue, and I had to parry her from moment to moment.

"Dalby, after we have been married for twenty-five years, I think you might at least entrust me with the name of your employer."

"Yes," I said heavily. There was nothing else I could do but put on the airs of the injured party. "But if you will think of what happened last night, and how Mr Wether's name came out, you'll see now why not."

Like any husband, I could see that the constant drip would force me in self-defence to invent a new cover story. I did not want to invent it in a hurry. There were reasons. I wanted to decide what I intended to do first. The new story when it came would have to be good. As a second attempt, it would have to be tailored to stand up not only to everything I was doing, but to Delicia Dobson and everything I might do. I wondered why wives, even against their own interests, forced husbands to invent cover stories. I was desperate.

I never quite understood why Margaret was particularly susceptible to humiliation. Perhaps the guilt in her life was that of having married me and thus having betrayed both her origins and background. Under the humiliation of the neighbours' supposition that I had a mistress, which I realized with amazement was even correct in a way, she produced a situation in which I had a chance to give up crime altogether.

It was a pity, from her point of view, that the opportunity she gave me came so late, and that my attitude to crime had changed in the meantime.

I had begun with a horror of crime. On the day I bought the vacuum cleaner and talked to the old man in the park, it seemed incredible that young vandals should stone ducks, and break trees, and not only rob the telephone booth on the corner but wreck it. I was as ready to talk about mindless evil as any pampered and insulated magistrate in those days, and accept the views that we should bring back the birch and the cat and hang them and flog them. But now I just wondered, why not? Underneath, I was thinking, or trying.

Why not declare war on a society in which one was rejected? Where one was born without choice, and where it was other people who claimed to own everything that could be seen, and who declared themselves to be of superior intelligence, by tests they had devised in their own style of language, and that they had the right to all the attractive rewards and to run things? Because it was like that ... Dobson, if someone like me had put him up to it, could have devised tests and examination papers written in his own Lockley dialect that all the legal and academic bright brains would have failed, without question.

A boy who failed his examinations at school, and was thrown out, as he knew he was going to be, at the earliest school-leaving age, knew already, no matter how dim he was, that he was not going to be the kind who owned a house, bought a car, attracted blondes, and took Riviera holidays. He was going to live at best in a council house, of which the rent, until he died, was going to be a constant load on his wages, and all his life he was going to have to be satisfied with the third-rate and fourth-rate. At the height of his prosperity, he would take his family to the seaside in a clapped-out car, seven years old, which someone else had run to death.

Hard facts? They were hard all right, from my worms-eye point of view, and I no longer blamed the youths for the telephone booths or the damage to the trees in the park. In my day, we had had a dream, Communism, Socialism, or some kind of political solution; but Stalin, and Churchill and Roosevelt, and all the cigar-smoking and pipe-smoking pontificating elder-politicians who had lost touch with what life was, had killed all that.

Margaret did not know, when she offered me the chance to get out of crime, that crime had come to seem to me the natural art form and expression of the deprived social classes.

"What do you intend to do?" she asked me a few days after the night of the flood.

In my mind, in those days, were excuses.

"What do I intend to do about what?" It was lunch-time again. We were at table in the dining-room, and I reflected that any husband who did not eat out was a captive audience, and subject to interview, or a prisoner under interrogation at lunch-times. It was the way that I felt it.

"We can't go on like this, Dalby."

"So you keep saying."

"Dalby, do you want me to leave you?"

I looked up. This was quite new. I saw something worse. There was a stillness. We looked at one another across the dining-table, two fifty-year-old faces.

She meant it. I felt horror.

"Where would you go?"

"I wouldn't like it, Dalby. It is the last thing. I could go to stay for a while with cousin Mavis."

I estimated the weight of her threat to go to stay for a while with her cousin. It was real. It was more dangerous than any forgotten-in-an-hour declaration that she would leave me for ever. It was real, and I sensed it. I was abject.

"Why do you want to do this, Margaret?" It was the kind of conversation we had not had for ten years or twenty.

"You will say it is my imagination if I say I get pitying looks, when I walk down the street, from the neighbours."

"No I don't. I've not said that."

She just looked. That kind of conversation did not include contradictions.

I succumbed. I asked for an armistice and terms. I was married to Margaret.

"What do you want me to do?"

"There is nothing you can do, except tell people the truth, and that is something you won't do."

"Well then?"

"We must move."

I thought: move. I had started everything to keep Margaret in that house, and I had produced the opposite of my intentions. It was that we had come to.

I felt relief.

Someday I would recover from the night of the flood. Someday ... if I had money and could do things. In the meantime, somewhere, in her room probably, but doing something I could not envisage, was Delicia Dobson. What could I do about her in the meantime? If we moved ... I had a feeling of the impossibility of everything. I remembered that night when I came home, when I was thinking of Delicia Dobson and was observed by a policeman as I stood looking at a car on a corner. I needed money. I needed the ability to act, for all things.

But move?

"To where?"

Margaret gave me the opportunity to give up crime. "To a small house in the country."

15

I DO NOT want to excuse violence.

But then I did not think of it as violence.

The country bus service radiated out in all directions. I looked at the state of the rural economy sometimes in those winter days. I looked at frost in the fields, and snow under hedgerows, from the bus, during slow winter journeys.

A new life. It had my own meaning. And a promise to Margaret.

On most days during those weeks I left after breakfast.

"I'll look at this cottage at Langton. If you have time, you can look at this small house at Brisley." It was an arrangement that looked sensible. It was a story that held water.

Then the country bus would leave the main road and make long detours. I would see, and later have much to tell about, the villages.

It would not last, but then it was not meant to last. A few weeks, I thought. Give me time. It was a way to live, a *modus vivendi*. Desperately, I thought: Give me time to build up my fortune. I did not see I had much choice about the way or the method.

I went to the cottages and to the villages to which I was supposed to go, and then I went on to the small towns. I watched her when we both came home in the evening, and I kept it going when she looked too dispirited.

"Remember that we can change the way they look," I encouraged her. "You don't have to be put off by the brown paint. We don't have to live as the poor lived." She knew I had some money, I did not say how much.

All the cottages that could be converted and modernized had been bought up round Lockley. She came home one day and said, "How do they live without water and electricity?" It gave me time. I knew that now it had to be one way or the other. I took the buses on to their destinations, to places like Gorham and Lipley and Fentham.

It had seemed to me for some time that if I did anything it would have to be in the small market towns. I looked at them and went from one to the other. It seemed to happen of its own accord, that I became methodical. I looked at the trade directories in the public libraries. It was strangely peaceful in a town where I was unknown, among the silence and books. In the banks, I inquired about facilities for cash since I was making a purchase and my account was not local. I did not only look at the customers, it was legitimate business.

Fentham was the place I worked first. I worked it out that there would have to be several. It was a small market town with a square. It might in fact have been one of the places where there could have been a cottage five miles out, without electricity and water and not on a bus route. It was the country factory on the outskirts that I looked at after I had been to the bank, and I watched people coming out, and I saw that there were under a hundred employees.

There was a lot of that empty, peaceful countryside around Lockley, where it was possible to travel miles on a bus, getting nowhere, where the country girls wore short skirts and there was television in the houses, but where things did not seem to change from one year to the next, and the places all seemed to have much the same name. I carried my big old brief-case with me when I went there on the bus on the Friday.

We were held up for a few minutes on the bus. A furniture van blocked the road, and by a cottage like those Margaret had gone to see there was a woman with weeping children among boxes and furniture of no value that was put by the roadside. Someone said, "An eviction." A policeman directed the bus round the van. I knew I was going to do it then. Until then I had not known I dared. I had been undecided, despite the preparations I had made and the things I had put in my brief-case.

When the bus came to Fentham, it ran through the narrow streets past small houses. At the small depot by the square, I got off. I went down to the Gents. I adjusted my coat and I looked into the brief-case at the bottle and blond wig. I wondered if it were good enough, then I thought I was being too elaborate. The wig was not even intended to be convincing. I came out of the Gents, and looked at the time. I walked around the square where the one traffic warden had nothing to do, and I looked in a window, seeing the reflections behind me in the glass as I pretended to examine agricultural machinery as though I intended to buy it.

I had been to Fentham before. The car was a little late that day. It drove into the square and across it and into a small alleyway cul-de-sac near the main street, where a sign said, No Parking. I looked at the man who drove it, who looked my age but was a little more frail since he had not been practising burglary through the winter. I had noticed how the car went to the alley with the No Parking sign. It was a weekly event, and he did it under the eye of the warden.

I walked around the square, and he got out of the car and picked up a black bag, and when he closed the car door he was the kind who always locked it. He nodded to the warden, who knew him, and crossed the corner of the square to the town's lively main street. With his small narrow black bag he looked like a man who was respectable and careful.

The main street ran along one side of the square and carried the heavy traffic through the town. It was narrow and had the usual shops such as a Boots and a Woolworth's, and was lined along its length with double white lines. If anyone were going to park in a no-parking area they were better in the alley than if they blocked all the traffic. The man whose hair was as thin as, and a little greyer than, mine crossed the street and went into the Westminster bank that was next to the Boots' branch.

I walked up the street past a tobacconist's, a hardware, and a tailor's. I did not cross the road but turned into a passage-way that was adjacent to Woolworth's. There was no access to the shop from the passage, and a brass plate on the entrance where it faced the street proclaimed a dentist's. Half way through the passage was a door that said, No Entry, while a stairway with a pointing hand led up to the dentist in his rooms above the shops. I went through the No Entry door which was not kept locked. It only led to the backs.

I had explored the town in detail when I had marked the man. The question had been how. I had traced his car back to a parking lot at the rural factory that made kinds of belting and netting. It had been parked in the small factory front right under the accounts department windows. There was no way at that end.

After I had gone through the No Entry door, I stopped in the passage. The man stayed an average of only seven minutes in the bank, and I had to work quickly. I stripped off the heavy dark coat I was wearing, and under it I wore a light-coloured mack with the collar turned down and the skirts and sleeves taped up. I took off the mack and put the heavy coat on first, then the mack on the outside. I left the brief-case where it was, but opened it and took out and put on the blond wig. Seen from a distance, I now looked a much heavier and bulkier young man. Seen from close-to, I was obviously in disguise, but it would be difficult for anyone to be at all precise about my age or my build or description. I took a wine-bottle from my brief-case, and a spare driving glove, and went out through the backs. I felt foolish. I also felt desperately frightened.

The dentist's yard led to a back alley through a door that I had to unbolt, though there was nothing there that could be stolen but a damp packing-case and a dustbin. The alley led past similar yards behind the shops and ended in a tall wooden door with a large slide-bolt on the inside and a line of barbed wire on top to discourage intruders. I was fortunate that there was no one in the alley. Had there been a van there delivering to the shops, I would have had to go back and reverse my disguise, and wait till the next week.

I unbolted the door at the end of the alley like a shop-assistant expecting delivery. In my pale coat and blond wig I hoped I might be taken, if anyone looked out of the rooms above the shops, for a storeman from Woolworth's. When I opened the large door to let a delivery van in, I found that the alley entrance, which served several backs, was blocked by a parked car. I stood waiting for the driver to return with something indistinguishable beneath my arm and what could have been a rag in my hand. From the door, I could look out only into a narrow section of the square and see people passing. The wait lasted three minutes. He was a little longer than normal on that day. I was lucky that no one came by me.

My hands were sweating and I felt sick. It was the first time since the war that I had done violence. I had nothing against the man, and I hoped that he, as well as the money, was covered by the firm's comprehensive insurance. I had no compunction about taking money from an insurance company if I could get it. Insurance could only be sold because thefts sometimes happened, and by producing one of the thefts I was benefiting the insurance company's business.

When the man appeared across the square, coming back from the main street, I drew back in the doorway. I slid the bottle from my arm to my right hand and held the spare driving glove in my left. The bottle was a brand of wine sold in a supermarket in a town to the east and that was not sold in Lockley. The driving glove had been given me by an aunt in Margaret's family who did her shopping in London, and it still bore the trademark. The man did not notice that the door behind his car was open. He was carrying his black bag as he came towards me looking at his car door and feeling in his pocket for the keys. I waited until he stooped to the door, then I emerged into the alley. I dropped the glove by the car, then I hit him on the head with the bottle.

It was all done very quickly. I was unlucky, but not very unlucky. There was a scream from the square, rather distant, uncertain, and female. The man did not go down as I expected when I hit him. I was not experienced, and I had not hit hard enough, but he dropped the bag and clung to the car. I stopped to pick up the bag, and remained stooped while visible. I remembered to drop the bottle, but he made a staggering motion towards me as I went off for the alley. He did not make it, and fell. I did not look back into the square, but went through and bolted the tall door behind me. I was running a definite and clear and calculated risk at that time.

The risk was that someone would come out of one of the yards into the alley. They would not have seen what had happened, but they would know about it shortly, and they would have seen me. There was also another, and finite, but lesser risk. It was that the dentist, or someone from his surgery, might choose that time, and that day of the week, to go down to his dustbin. My disguise would be helpful for the first, but if I were changing at the time, it would not be any use for the second. I went quickly up the alley past the back yards of three shops. I turned again into the dentist's yard, and bolted the door. I crossed it quickly because at that point I was visible again to the upper windows and backs including those of the next street. When I got into the passage I put my foot against the back of the door that on the other side said No Entry. Along the backs, from the square, I could hear some commotion and shouting.

Two minutes later, I emerged from the dentist's into the main street. I was again middle-aged, and I was dressed in dark clothes. I was carrying a bulky brief-case, but it was obvious that I had been to the dentist's, for I had a handkerchief in my hand which I applied to my lips and I kept my head bent.

A woman came past from the square, dragging a child. "An accident," she was saying, looking at the child as she passed me. "You should not stand and gape at such things." Men in the street were looking towards the square. I looked for a police car but did not see one until later, passing quite slowly behind an overladen van and snarled up in traffic. I crossed the road and took my handkerchief from my face. I believed I had been successful.

It was afterwards, as I was walking away, that I felt a reaction and was weak at the knees. I was away. The descriptions the police would get would be, "A blond young man", or "A man in a wig", but it was the risk that I felt, the time when I went back up the alley, and when I was changing behind the door in the dentist's passage. I lived it again. I thought of the four or five other similar robberies I would have to do in nearby or more distant towns and small places, and I thought that somehow, though I did not see how, I must eliminate such risks. I walked away from the square and around the back of the block to the bus station, where I took a bus to another town, not directly to Lockley. I improved my technique slightly, by thinking about it as I sat in the bus; but though I wished to develop the art to the state I had burglary, I could see no way to eliminate all risk.

It was some time before I thought of the man I had hit. It was not until I had gone down to a Gents again in the new town and counted the money, which was as much as I could expect from a firm that did not employ a Securicor van, a little less than £1,000. I was glad I had not hit him too hard, yet I knew I had under-estimated the force required for the blow and if I wished to be safe I must hit the next man a little harder. I could not afford the risk there would have been had he grabbed me. I had the knowledge and experience of life, and I had to get it right. It was not my fault that, as a technician, unqualified and unemployed, I had to strike out at the men who ran firms. I thought of him swaying dizzily as he grabbed at the car. It was men exactly like him who had refused me employment in offices. They were not responsible for me, they claimed, and though I knew that a blow on the head would not help them, I told myself that they were to blame when I, as a technician, went free lance.

I thought I had made a start, a beginning, and went back to Margaret.

16

It DID NOT help the agony of the last dying phases of our Derrington Drive life.

I could not solve the problem of how far I was responsible for myself and other people. In a foolish way, I caught myself wishing I could tell people what I was doing, and explain why. Of course it was impossible, I could see that.

I looked at Margaret's eyes as we both sat in, the evening after we had been out all day. The phase of looking for a cottage was not over. It should have been, but she could see no way of going on living in Derrington Drive. What she did was to declare that the search was impossible, then to think of the neighbours and of the situation they thought that we had created between us, and then start looking again.

At the moment, she was in the despairing phase of the mood, and my sympathy was genuine. I wished I could tell her what I was doing. I wished I could say, "There's a way out."

"You aren't any help," she said.

I was struck constantly by the way in which, to her, our life had become like a nightmare. Like everyone else, I had read George Orwell's *1984*, and seen his theory that everyone had some particular dread or dislike that could break them. In his case it was being eaten alive by rats. Margaret's had happened by chance. Neither of us had known, or could have foreseen in advance, that it was to live in a middle-class street and to be despised and subject to the pity of neighbours.

She could not help feeling superior to the townspeople, the Godlings, the McFarlanes, the Belfonts, with their houses that they regarded as the end of everything, their gardens, their cars. It was not just that the whole street would have been lost in the lands once owned by her fathers, but to her it was innate. She had been able to tolerate them and made a life with me there, but that was when I was at least their equal in making money. She could pretend equality with them, but know in her heart that they were smaller, and that neither she, nor for that matter I, was of their class.

Not to be equal to them, to have to live with them but in a lesser way than them, in a poverty that was visible in things like old paint and old curtains, and then to have them pity her because there was evidence now that her husband was unfaithful, was a thing she could never have dreamed of until it happened; and it went deep, so deep that I could now see that it was something she could never properly express, like the worst kind of nightmare.

"I went to look at a cottage today too, dear."

Her eyes, which had a look of despair in them that I had not seen before, looked as though she had lost faith that there could be hope any more in what I did.

I had to hint something. "I met Mr Wether in the town on the way back. He was in a good mood, and he said something new. He wants me to do some work in the daytime." I thought she would jump at the news. I could afford to say I had more money and was employed in the daytime.

I also thought of something else—in the way my plans were going. In case her mood suddenly changed, and she hit out in some new way, instead of looking at the cottages that her ancestors had given to serfs, I had to let her know I was engaged in the daytime.

With scorn, she said, "Mr Wether?" She was helpless.

"It's the easiest thing to call him," I said. "Without the money from him, I would be really unemployed, and neither of us could go about freely."

It was almost too much for her imagination, as it was for all people who had money, to know what it was like not to be able to afford bus-fares, but I saw her taken-aback as she tried it.

She did try. That was the difference between her and the Belfonts.

"What was the cottage you saw like?" she said.

"You wouldn't like it because of the smell of the pigs in the farm that is next door." As it happened I was truthful. "It is really three rooms stuck on to the end of the farm, next to the barn, and there are signs of rats in the woodwork."

She saw the picture. I did not have to describe the cobbled yard and the manure-heap in detail.

"We need more money, Dalby." It was a despair-cry.

I thought before I spoke. Everything had to fit in, and I had not yet completed the new plans I was making.

"We might get it, if you are prepared to put up with things just a little while longer." It is possible that I sounded as though I asked her to help me.

She looked again, like a question, but not believing.

"I just told you. I met Mr Wether. There is something he wants me to do in town. He'll entrust me with new work."

She did not want to decry my efforts. I could see what she thought. She said, "It will bring a few pounds in."

"I might tell you more about Mr Wether. But you will have to stop asking his name, if I tell you."

I had temporized since the night of the flood. At the same time I had thought out the angles, and I believed I could tell her a story.

She listened on that night.

"I lied to you about his name," I said. "Have you asked yourself, dear, why I had to?"

"It's not long since you never lied to me at all, Dalby."

I began to play God. It was really the first time.

"I told you the truth when I said he was a builder. What I didn't tell you was that he was one of the builders who, if his name came out, would produce a scandal in Lockley. It hasn't been easy, dear. Can you keep a secret this time, if I tell you that the payments from income he couldn't account for were bribes to the council?"

Margaret's eyes narrowed. "Dalby, how are you mixed up in nefarious business of this kind?"

"Agricultural land is worth £500 an acre. Passed for building, it's worth £5,000. The only difference is where the lines are drawn in County Planning. A committee chairman and two officials. What do you want to know, my employer's name, or what he does? I suppose that I could, but I won't tell you both things. If it ever came out, it would wreck both him and me now."

I wondered how far I would have to play God, and she looked away to the window where the curtains were drawn and stopped asking questions. I wondered if there were a law that said that if a man had a morality that was different from the norm, he must deceive other people.

It was a common enough scandal. It was the way things were rigged. To take advantage of it, even if you did not pay bribes, you had to own, or be in a position to buy, the land in the first place. In her father's house, when I had first gone there, much of the talk had been about land values. I had chosen the subject. It just happened that, apart from the careful language of the newspaper reporting, there had been no scandal of that kind in Lockley for a few years.

"You told me that his trouble was the bills he left in workmen's overalls and sent to the laundry."

"I thought you might guess. It would be a little out of scale to go next door and tell the truth to the McFarlanes."

I watched her as I hit the right note. It was as though she wore a new face. There was something different about Margaret. It was hope, or something a little like it.

I was not quite prepared when she said, "Will you make much money, Dalby?"

I thought, then I said, "Several thousand."

I waited to see if she hit the roof, and she did not. I admired her. There was not a flicker of her eyes, and I watched her expression not changing. When I asked, "Do you want me to give it up and retire to a cottage?" she showed just a shade of impatience. I expected to be cross-questioned, but it was not the way it took her. It was more that she was silent for a while, and then moved to a new scale of thinking. She seemed to contemplate something inside herself, and then it was as though she had changed gear.

I did not expect the things she said, but they were much better than the things I thought she might say. Her first question went very nearly to the heart of the problem.

"Dalby, when you have got this money, how are you going to account for it?"

I wished I knew how I was going to account for it. I was having enough difficulty accounting for it to Margaret.

I hesitated, and said, "To the neighbours?"

"Yes."

"We are going to move," I said. "You said so."

"To a cottage, yes. They would understand that. But unless we move away from Lockley altogether, how will you account for a move to another good house?"

I showed her I did not know. The logical thing to do, when I had got enough money, would have been to move right out of the district. But for me that would have meant leaving Delicia Dobson, and I could see that she too thought it impossible, because it would take me away from Mr Wether's employment.

I said, "We will think of something."

She looked at me as though I were a child, and then as though she made up her mind to tell me something.

"Uncle Kingsman is dying."

"What?"

"Uncle Kingsman has cancer." She was impatient again. It was not only the news, of which I had heard some indications, though not in that abrupt way, when she told me of cousin Mavis's last letter. It was more as though I were being slow, and ought to see the connection.

"You mean he might leave you something... ?"

"You know he won't do that." She looked at me as though I were the cause, which was true enough. If she had not married me, and had remained close to her uncle like her unmarried cousin Mavis, she might have inherited a share of his fortune.

"But the people here don't know it," she said.

I thought: Margaret.

I looked at her with a little wonder. It was not just that she had accepted what I had said regarding the white-collar crimes, she had entered into complicity with me.

"That would certainly be a way of explaining how we could afford things like a car and a house and a new way of life," I said. I only hoped she would let me do the lying.

"You get the money, and I will explain it," she said.

I tried to think if it were I who was responsible for Margaret agreeing to crime. I could see that I was in a way. If I had kept my job with Lee and Lawson's, she would never have agreed to lies and complicity. She would have retained the Derrington Drive housewives' outlook that all criminals should be heavily punished. In their righteousness, and their belief in rectitude, and their ideas about how criminals should be punished, they were worse than the men.

Yet it was not for the loss of my respectable work for Lee and Lawson's that I could be said to be directly responsible. It was as though, by deceiving Margaret, and creating a reality for her, in the form of my stories about Mr Wether, which she had to believe, I had become much more responsible for her than I ever had been. And I could see no way out of this. It was true, I always felt now, that a man had a right to choose his own morality, but I came back to what I had been thinking some time before. I denied the logic of it. Surely people who acted in a conventionally moral way were just as responsible for the end results of their actions as those who did not. It was they who were responsible for what happened to Margaret. But I still felt uneasy.

It was the risk of daylight robbery that came to me every time I thought of the money, now in two tin boxes in the pit under the garage. After Fentham, I was planning an affair involving the taking of an antique shop in Gorham. No thief could have been more aware of the likelihood of a slip.

"If your uncle dies conveniently, it would do no harm to say that you have hopes and expectations." For a moment I felt about Margaret as though she were an abstruse problem in algebra.

I knew she would want to do the telling herself, when it was anything to do with her family. I was decisive. "You can tell the McFarlanes."

17

I THOUGHT: DELICIA DOBSON.'

Delicia Dobson had been the inspiration for my daylight robberies. Did other criminals have to feel, as I did, that what they were doing was right? I felt a craving need for Delicia, for her poverty, and even for Dobson.

It may seem incredible that at this time I took Delicia out in a hired car.

I even prepared the ground for it with Margaret. I could afford no more slips.

"I am not sure I should have worked my way into his favour as much as I have," I said doubtfully on an occasion when I had been out all day. "Mr Wether's affairs are so complicated, and he is starting to use me as errand boy in his delicate private matters; and there is nothing for us in that, as there is in his business."

"You can't choose what you do for an employer," Margaret said. "Dalby, you should not be lazy."

I let it go as though I had accepted her reprimand. Later she asked me, "What private matters?"

"What?"

"You said Mr Wether was employing you in his private affairs."

"It is in connection with his illegitimate daughter, who, it turns out, is a poor child, and half-paralysed," I said. "I wish I could tell you."

My sole intention in saying things of this kind to Margaret was to cover my tracks in case I was seen with Delicia Dobson.

I dropped other words from time to time. I did not have any coherent plan about it, except to ensure that whatever new accidents transpired I would be able to blame what I had been seen to have done on my new, more important and more involved Mr Wether. I even thought that if I were arrested committing a daylight robbery somewhere I would be able to tell Margaret I had not been there at the time but that I could not tell the police where I was because I had been working for Mr Wether. It would give her some comfort, I thought, if she imagined I had been wrongfully arrested. But I chiefly used Mr Wether for more practical purposes:

"I drove a car again today, dear."

"I hope you remembered to renew your driving licence."

"I did. But it felt strange to be driving. Mr Wether told me to go somewhere in a hurry, and when I said, 'How?' he told me to take the firm's car."

I had not in fact driven a car again at that time, but I was contemplating doing so, though not in the vicinity of Derrington Drive. I was really, all the time, frightened.

I took elaborate precautions when I did use a car. There was a perfectly good car-hire firm on the west side of the town, nearest to Derrington Drive, but I did not use this firm, Limbers. Instead, by bicycle, I went off to a garage on the road to the east. When the man in charge saw my driving licence and remarked that I was quite close to Limbers, I said yes, but I had bought a car from Mr Limber once; he seemed to think that quite explained it.

I was feeling my way. I wanted to cover all contingencies, and probably I told some lies that were unnecessary. At the same time, I developed a taste for it. I liked to involve people in a new reality, which was quite consistent with all they saw and heard, yet which was one that I had invented. It was an art which made me wonder what reality was, and I considered how tenuous was most people's hold on it, and how, perhaps, what most people thought of as reality was not so at all. Reality was something else; accepted reality was merely a matter of people's desires and customs.

I thought at first when I hired a car that I might use it for one of the robberies I was working on, some of which, since I could only work where the opportunity existed, took me quite long distances and into the next county. I rejected the use of the car for that purpose in the end. Once I used it to go to a town near where I proposed to work, and then went by bus. My get-away was always safer, as a man who was obviously too old and too respectable to commit violent crime, on a bus. The use of a car for that type of crime was far too much what the police would have expected. I did not dare most things.

I used the car to take Delicia out for the day. I felt that I had to get not only her but me out that room of hers when I visited her. I could hardly push her in a wheel-chair through the streets of Lockley. To hire a car and take her out in it, at least as far away as the neighbouring seaside towns, was the only way. Even then, I avoided the towns as far as possible in case someone from Lockley should see me, and sought the quieter areas along the coast. Delicia's own sense of geography was so erratic that when I took by-roads and lanes, and avoided all the main roads, she did not know the difference.

Though it was early in the year, there were some days when it was good to go out, provided the sun shone. I took her to places I knew were sun-traps, with what warmth there was reflecting from the rocks and the sea, sheltered beneath the high cliffs. Even in winter it seemed like summer there for a few hours at midday; and it made it all the more extraordinary for her who did not know how rare such places or occasions were.

"How do I know you will bring her back?" Dobson said the first time I drove a car up their lane and calmly stopped at the front door. I had developed a relationship with Dobson that would have been impossible had it not been for my own

Ramsden Bottom background; a remark of this kind was not as mad as it seemed, nor did it quite mean what it implied in our conversations that were almost diplomatic manoeuvres.

I had told Delicia I would come "someday", when the weather was fine, but I do not think she had believed me. We had to wait between the door and the stairs while she became accoutred to go out, an elaborate process for her, though I was nervous of the car standing outside.

"Why should you worry if I don't bring her back?" I said. "Aren't you always complaining of her trouble and expense? I would think you would be grateful if I took her off in the car and did not come back."

"Yerse," he said, giving me a sideways look. "And then you could have her and draw her Assistance."

Delicia's Assistance was part of what they lived on. I doubted if Social Security themselves understood the economy of the household. I took the opportunity.

"Have you spoken to the landlord about what I told you, putting in a new bathroom downstairs?" I had the money to do it.

"I can't see the landlord. I owe six weeks' rent." He gave me another look.

I had begun to see and to realize that I was not going to be able to put in a bathroom for Delicia while she lived with her father, and this was a dire blow. It was not the rent, merely that the landlord would be reluctant to act, to seek planning permission; and negotiations would be impossible conducted through Dobson. I was very far from being the ordinary, anonymous benefactor, and I did not dare to come out in the open.

"I told you to see him."

"I owe six weeks' rent. I've not got it."

The result of the conversation was that I had to pay him six weeks' rent, not to see the landlord to whom he would tell some sly and heavily-angled story, but in order to take out Delicia for her car-ride.

It crossed my mind that if I really wanted to do anything for Delicia, my aim should be not to build her a bathroom, but to get her away from her father. Even the Welfare State could have provided better for her had it not been for him. But at that moment she came down, calling for us to help her.

It was the first time I had seen Delicia dressed to go out, and as I held the gate while Dobson helped her along the path, I was shocked. Dressed as Dobson dressed her, she was not only a cripple, she was ugly.

It was only after we had been driving in the car for a while that I was brought back to her by the animation of her face, and her innocence, and the way the passing countryside entranced her. She was something beneath it all. She "came through". To her, the whole world was brand new, the fields and the hedgerows. I had said "This afternoon," and she said, "Will we go to a café for lunch?" The whole drive was an ecstatic and extraordinary adventure.

Not a café if I could help it. I had seen her more or less naked, but other people hadn't. "It's such a nice day, don't you think? I thought we'd go for a picnic."

"Oh, yes!" She was delighted with the idea, yet disappointed that she could not do both things at once. We would be far too conspicuous. I was sorry it had to be a picnic, not a wild café lunch, but I could see no alternative until I could buy her some new clothes. Fortunately she was distracted.

"Oh, look, lambs!" she said, like a child finding something she had seen only two or three times in her life. She made the best of it, and it was enough of an experience, truly, just to be riding in a car. "Once we went on a picnic from the school, in the school bus, but it rained." Holding on to the car seat, she chattered and behaved a little like a child on a school treat, and she must have realized it, for she said, "When the education people sent me to that school, I went in a taxi." She made efforts to appear like a woman of the world and constantly revealed her total lack of experience. Yet she knew it and laughed bitterly.

I wondered, in a kind of appalled and touched and still-determined way, what I could do with her. I might buy her a coat and a dress, there had been enough women in my family for me to be able to deal with that kind of thing, and make her look right, but I could not do the rest. What I wildly hoped for was in some way to bring her out, and get her accustomed to dealing with the world, doing things for herself, so that she could eventually get a job. It was almost impossible to see how I could do it unless I brought a woman in somewhere.

She had never seen a place like the one we went to, but there was nothing very surprising in that. Even on a summer Sunday not a high proportion of tourists found it, and in my choice of a place where a narrow lane led down to the beach under some cliffs, and in the kind of food and drink I had bought, I was trying to make up to her for not having taken her to a café. She was astonished at the brilliance from the sea and the way the sunlight reflected down from the cliffs, so early in the year. She used the highest praise she knew, "It is like television. It's like a desert island."

A desert island would not have provided the bottles and the foods of which she did not know the names, except perhaps in the advertisements. But then, as I had discovered, she watched the advertisements closely. They were a window to an enchantment she thought was the real world.

Sitting on the sand, with her back against a rock and looking at the glitter of the sea, she said, "Oh, I wish..."

"What do you wish?" I asked her.

"Oh, it doesn't matter. I don't know what I wish," she said. Her thin, pale features were animated, and she looked at a seagull that was circling and calling. I thought, how symbolic. Perhaps I over-did it, with even the small amount of alcohol

I gave her, and the heat of the sunlight, the air and a place the like of which she did not know existed any nearer than the South Seas, for after a while she became morbid, waving a hand with an anguished and fey air.

"I suppose you come here often?"

I had told her that I had a wife and a family.

"No. We used to, but my children are grown up and have gone away. My wife can't, because we don't have a car now. I was only able to bring you today because my employer, who is a member of our Society, said I could and let me use the firm's car." I tried to make her get a grip on my reality.

I used the same story about the car that I had used with Margaret, but without thought. Delicia was not Margaret, and there did not have to be any great consistency in the stories I told her. Sometimes there did not have to be any at all.

"I don't suppose I will ever come here again."

"You will, because I'll bring you."

"Oh, you might do it, sometime."

"I will, perhaps the next time we have a fine day."

She looked back towards the road and the cliffs. We had passed a house on the way down. To me it had looked like a holiday home that was shut up for the winter, but she had not noticed that. She said, "I suppose some people live here, in places like this. I have to live with my father, and when he dies, I'll have to go into a Home. I'll have nowhere else to go to." Her thin face was screwed up.

"You could do something about that, Delicia," I said to her gently. What else could I do? I talked to her lengthily.

She thought about it, about the possibility of getting out of her situation by her own efforts. She knew it was possible, and she must have been told about it, in terms of qualifications and training for jobs, at some stage in her education. I tried to imagine what she thought when she could not think of, but only sense, the advantages that other children had, of parents who were familiar with the requirements of

131

intellectual work, of parents who, quite simply, could and did read, and kept books in their houses. She played with the sand with her fingers. "Not me," she said eventually. I saw that she meant it.

There did not seem much point in continuing the conversation. I had seen what a performance it was to get her out of the house, and could guess Dobson's reaction if he were asked to do it three nights a week; to accompany her, to bring her home, and do all the other things he would have to do to get her to night school. The whole thing was impossible.

"I would help."

"Oh, you," she said. She became aware of me and said, "Do you want to make love to me on the beach here?"

I did not. I began to collect all the things to put back into the car so that we could go for another drive before I took her home. I could not face how it would look, even though there was no one there to see it, in the sunlight and the air by the sea, between a crippled girl and a man of fifty. It was bad enough in her room at home, though even there we did not make love completely. I was oddly not that way.

Driving up the narrow lane between the cliffs, I noticed the house she had mentioned. It was shut up and had an unoccupied look. There was a For Sale sign. I pointed it out to her, but she seemed regretful, not pleased, and said, "Perhaps it's not possible for anyone to live here."

I did not think much of it at the time, only later. When we came to the cliff-top road, the sign to the place said "Penfold", and I turned left along the rest of the cliff road to let her see the National Trust headland; but it was only scenery, for of course she could not walk there. We turned round and got back at six o'clock, as I had promised to Dobson.

"Did you go to see your landlord?" I asked him.

"He wants more rent," he said. "He said, who'd want to rent a cottage like this, with two bathrooms? He said you'd have to pay him to do it, and if you wanted to do anything about it, you should see the council yourself, and get all the plans passed." Dobson spoke as though he were glad of misfortune, as though things had to stay as they were.

It was very difficult for me to help Delicia. Quite apart from whether I should, it was a question if I could. It was as impossible as I had thought it might be.

He became busy helping Delicia to get back upstairs to her room, and I had to take the car back and cycle home. I felt thwarted and saddened by the news that it was no use going further with any plans for improving the cottage. I was not in a position to take official steps, like getting plans passed by the council, when officially I was myself just an unemployed man. I could never put my name to any papers.

"I brought her back anyway," I said, as though to say something positive when I was about to go out, but he had failed in something himself and it did not improve him.

He was in a black mood. I suspected that he had hatched some plan for himself out of the proposed alterations, and it had not come off because he had been too devious about it and taken the wrong line with the landlord. He had his arm round Delicia and was nominally helping her up the stairs, but he said, in her hearing, "Don't expect me to thank you for that." He was needlessly vicious. "Any time, you can have her."

I learned later that what had happened was that he had asked a woman to live with him, but she had refused to take on Delicia. At the time I could only tell, to my surprise, that he seemed to mean it.

I went out to go home. I was on the verge of creation.

18

I WONDERED HOW, faced with it, other people would introduce the great events of their life? Modesty, I imagine, would be the best way. The artlessness, the ingeniousness that conceals art, the kind of thing of which all the professional writings in the Lockley library seem to consist. I can well imagine: "At this time I was knocking down people in the street and taking their money, and yet to me..."

Or: "It is little understood that while crime may seem to fill the criminal's mind, the actual time he devotes to it..."

I could well use this kind of language. I would like to say "Look," to myself. I would like to say, "See, there is nothing difficult about this, just recount the events as they happened. They are enough in themselves, and all that is required is that you should be quite honest."

Shades of the psycho-analyst's couch.

The urge to the professional, the atmosphere of the court. Is this what I am doing, telling myself I am a "bad" man?

I would not mind that.

I would love to be called bad. And bold. And sinful.

I wonder how many criminals have done that in court, and made themselves out to be bad, and taken their sentences, and, when the judge has described them, and given them the importance that inside themselves they most feared they did not have, been truly grateful.

I resist these temptations.

I drove towards the sea. I tried to follow the same route I

had taken with Delicia, but I missed one of the turnings. It was still important, I thought, that I should not be seen driving a car by anyone I knew, yet in some ways I was almost past caring.

Do I have to explain that? I do not think so.

I drove for a while in the country between Lockley and Derrington Drive and the sea. It was only a matter of the lanes, some of which I appeared to have forgotten. Then I came out at a turning I did know. I went on to the sea, and sometimes the sun came out on the cliffs and the moorland ahead. The weather had deteriorated, but it did not matter when I was inside the car, and I did not expect to do much outside it.

I was alone. I was not very clear about what I was doing. If I had had to explain it to myself, I would have said I had taken the car for my own pleasure. Or that would probably have been what I would have said to someone else, if there had been anyone I might, even remotely, have confided in. To myself, I don't think I would ever have used the word "pleasure".

I was not quite as I was. I had hired the car before, true, but that had been to take Delicia out, and I could take her out in no other way. It had not crossed my mind to hire a car for myself before, though I had had the money to do it. And I had only a vague sense of purpose.

I am trying to trace the development of an idea. To me, it has importance.

I drove out on to the coast road on the cliffs, and came out not far from the headland. I could see Penfold almost at once from where I came out on the cliff road, and I looked for the house. It was not in an exposed position, as it would have been had I been able to see it at once, so it was a little while before I saw it. I slowed down when I did. There was no traffic on the cliff road at that time of year, so I was able to drive for a while at about twenty miles an hour, and look at the country. It was open, and I did not object to it. It was not quite so remote as it looked; to anyone who had a car almost nowhere was in England. In fact, I rather liked it.

I rather liked the house, too. It was clearly more expensive than anything I had envisaged having. It was the kind of thing Margaret and I had sometimes said we would retire to, but only on our best days. I was a little put off by that. It is an illusion that a thief does not know the value of money. I knew the value of money more than anyone else, for I was taking more risks to get it. All the same, I kept my eye on the house as I drove round it, and then down the lane, and came to the drive. I looked carefully for the For Sale sign, and saw it was still there. I thought that the owner would have to keep it there until summer if he was asking a good price. I wondered if he would compromise, and take the benefit of a quick sale for a cheap one.

I opened the gate of the house and drove into the drive. I could only look at the outside, and I did a little of that. I had no key or permission to view. I had by no means got that far.

I spent a time standing by the car and looking at the view. I had done that when we were buying Derrington Drive, on my own, and then pretended I was seeing it for the first time when I went there with Margaret. It was more windy that day than when I went there with Delicia, and after a while I sat in the car in the garden, which had more or less run to seed. I was not particularly worried in case anyone came along to ask me what I was doing. I was a possible purchaser taking a look. But there was no one in sight who might say anything, and anyway, you could always do that with a For Sale house.

After a while, I got out a pencil and paper. This was a part of the evolution of the idea. I did not think it was a good idea. I did not think it would work. In fact I was pretty sure it was mad, and I meant even by my standards. I was not very sure what I was going to do with the pencil and paper. I looked out of the side of the car at the house, and saw how it was split-level, with its back in the hillside, and how a path came down from the upper level to the lower, that included a garage; it was that kind of a house. I thought: It is too damned expensive. I found that that was what the paper and pencil were for, to disprove my idea.

I drove the car back to the garage and cycled home. I thought about reality on the way. I did not really believe in reality either. At best, the only definition of reality was someone else's opinion. I looked at it in connection with the houses of Derrington Drive, and I thought. What the hell. It was stupid. It was a false line of argument, but I wondered what was reality, and I wondered if there was any reality that people truly believed. When I went into the house and ate with Margaret, and told her I had had a busy day on Mr Wether's business, I thought that reality was a chair and a cup, and some food, and a table.

I had sleepless nights for some time after that. I lay awake in bed thinking. I had had plans, but they had been vague plans. Now I saw an opportunity. I went to sleep after midnight. When I awoke at three, I thought my new plans were monstrous. When I awoke again at five, I thought they had the beauty of genius and were quite simple. When I awoke again in daylight, I did not know what I was thinking.

I did nothing the next day. I rode on a bus to a place called Fidley, and went into the banks and looked in the streets to see if I could see any money unguarded or being carried by hand there. Nothing came of it. In the vast majority of places nothing came of my inquiries when I made them in that way, but I could not think of a better.

In the *Sunday Times* Colour Supplement, I read an article about a judge. There was an artist's impression of him in his robes as he sentenced a jewel thief. I noticed how the thief was made to look shifty and hangdog. The judge looked knowing and human and righteous. I wondered about reality again. I decided that reality was a judge's invention. The jewels were stones that had been found in the ground, I imagined by black workers who were paid a pittance to work in a hole in what had once been their tribal ground. I imagined that it was the judge who convinced the thief and made him look shifty. It was the judge's robes and the pomp that made the proceedings look righteous. I could see no reason why the jewels should be regarded as the property of the judge, or the thief, or the man with the innocent belief that he owned them.

On the Monday, I hired the car and drove out to the house again. It was called Penfolds. It was isolated, and anyone who lived there would have the advantage, or disadvantage, that they would have no near neighbours. I had stopped on the way to get the key and an order to view from the agents. I let myself in, and walked from one empty room to another looking at the sea and the coast from the windows. I tried to imagine what the place would be like on a hot summer's day, when the people came down to the cove and walked on the cliffs, the lane congested with cars that came down and could find no parking. It would be different, I saw, with a gale from the south, when the rain obscured the cliffs in the depths of the winter.

I thought I was mad. I thought I was theorizing, and looking at houses. Between the theory, the house, the cove that Delicia liked, the garden and the view of the sea that I wanted, was a gap. I wondered how I could even start to make the moves that would close it.

That evening, when I got home, talking to Margaret over the meal table, like any husband mentioning details of his day's work, I said to Margaret, "How would you like to meet Mr Wether's illegitimate daughter?"

It felt strange, this time, to be talking in terms of a reality that was my own, artificial, creation.

"Dalby, why on earth should I want to meet that girl?" Margaret said.

It was the answer I expected, and I left it.

I wondered about Margaret. She had heard the stories I

told. She had the money I brought, and she knew there was more. We were waiting for her uncle to die, so that she could say she had come into a little money and explain to the neighbours. With regard to any physical evidence, she had seen Delicia's television; but she had never met Mr Wether, nor seen him. I wondered if people wanted to confirm the reality they believed in.

"What made you make such an extraordinary suggestion?" Margaret said.

"I don't know," I said. "The opportunity is there. I imagined you might have some curiosity. It was foolish of me. I can quite understand that you don't want to be involved in any of Mr Wether's business."

I could see Margaret struggling with herself and wondering if curiosity were a good enough reason. She knew the girl was illegitimate, and had, from the time she had had her television in the house. I had described her to Margaret once as "a poor working-class girl in a bad way." Now I said, "You'd better not anyway."

"Why not?"

"She doesn't know she's illegitimate or whose daughter she is. You might let it slip."

"Dalby, I'm as tactful as you are."

I was interested in this curious belief of Margaret's. Like most people with strong feelings and opinions she was clumsy and heavy-footed as a liar, and at the same time convinced, since she could not imagine anyone doubting her word, that she was an exceptionally good one.

"Do you want to meet her, or don't you?" I said mildly. "Forgive me, dear, if I don't quite understand you."

"Yes," she said. She put on an appearance of being rash. "I am tired of this house and this street." The justification appeared. "Almost anything would make a change." She looked worried that there was nothing moral to validate her actions, but said, "Yes. Though you make the girl sound wretched, I'll meet her."

It seemed that people did wish to confirm the reality they believed in. Margaret wanted to confirm the reality of Mr Wether.

"If you can be in the High Street at noon tomorrow, I'll pick you up and take you to lunch. I'll be driving the firm's car."

I thought Mr Wether might be more real to Margaret if she rode in the firm's car and had lunch with his daughter.

I tried to think what I was doing, and whether I was pandering to a dream, or if I thought that it would work and I meant it. It was art. It was the art of life. It was pure art. It is astonishing how people sometimes deceive themselves. It was the outcome of my thinking and experience so far that I thought of reality as a thing some people created.

I suppose that if I were quite sure about reality, I would not need to write this.

19

I TRIED IT out. That was me all right. In some ways, in so far as anyone can see himself, I can see it was all of what I was. I lacked the detail and the academic side and the learning of science, but I had got the principle. Faced with anything I did not know, I would try it out, on a small scale.

"Don't tell her," I said to Dobson when we were waiting on the stairs, "but I am taking her out to lunch today—with my wife."

Dobson said, "What?" I watched him to see how my reality worked. In fact, he was sitting on the lower stairs, and I stood in the hall. If I had been primarily interested in people as "characters", which I take to be their differences, and not the primary truths that unite them, I would say that Dobson was a man who would never stand if he could sit.

"I'm taking Delicia to meet my wife," I said, putting it about as simply as I could. "It is time that she met her."

Dobson said something that in Cockney would be "Cor", but in Lockley came out as a more colloquial expletive.

"Why do you say that?" I said.

"You're not going to let your wife see her?"

"Why not?" I was definitely interested to know if he had any reasons.

He had not. All he said was, "I can think of some wives..." then he seemed just to sit there and ponder.

I pondered too. I wanted to know if it would work, and if not just why not. I would have to handle it, I could see that.

"Mr Dobson," I said reprovingly, "we are respectable people."

That was at least one reality that I stuck to and held. I had only expected trouble with it when Delicia was ready and we got her down into the car and I drove off.

"No picnic today," I said blithely as I took a turning from the lane.

"What are we going to do?" She did not know what the turn meant, and looked ready for anything. Last time out in the car had been a good one. It was time reality intruded.

"We are going to pick up my wife and take her to a restaurant as well."

I only caught a glimpse of her face. "Oh, no!" escaped her involuntarily. She looked shattered. I felt sorry about that. I had never been good at being cruel to be kind. Some people seemed to like it.

"It's necessary," I said.

"Necessary?" she said passionately. "Why is it necessary? I can't meet your wife. Let me go home. I don't want to."

"Now don't be silly, dear, it's all right."

"No it isn't."

Anyone would have thought we had been to bed together, from the fuss she was making. I thought about it hard. Perhaps what we had done was the equivalent of going to bed for her.

"You'll survive," I told her, with an attempt to be cheerful.

She did not find it easy to be cheerful. She kept badgering me to turn the car round and take her home. I felt a shrewd insight into that. I did not think she was afraid Margaret would be jealous of her, or nasty, with, so far as Margaret knew, no reason. She just felt she was not up to it, that she would be far out-classed and show up badly; and about that she had reason.

There was one thing about having a cripple for a girl-friend, she could not just demand to be set down to walk. Besides, it did not take long to be back in the town again by a circular route, and I approached the place where I had to pick up Margaret. When I saw her, I did have something of the feeling of a juggler who had to keep two balls in the air during his whole act. I told myself I must not look at it that way. I must relax and not push things. Either the whole thing would go, or it would not.

"Margaret, this is Delicia." I had two car doors open on a no-waiting line at the corner of the High Street. "Do you want her to get out and go in the back, or will you ride there until we get to the road-house?" Margaret eyed me and the girl and the car. It looked all right. I knew it would. One glance at Delicia from Margaret, and Delicia could not be seen as a rival. As I drove off I reflected that a lot of wives had made that mistake, but it was not the kind of thought to be expressed for their consumption. Relax, I kept telling myself, relax. You are only here to see what happens. That is all you are here for.

"Has Dalby known you long, Miss Dobson?" Margaret asked. It was not only the politeness of making a new acquaintance's first contact, it was the compulsion a woman like Margaret had not to notice she was in a car, to be oblivious of a moving world, and to make conversation.

"No," said Delicia, who clearly was frightened.

"A little while," I said. "Since I have been calling on her on behalf of the Philanthropic Society." I thought it natural to lay a little stress on this, to remind Margaret of the cover story I had told her I was operating on Mr Wether's behalf. "Delicia's mother is elsewhere, you know, and she lives with her father."

Driving, I could only glimpse Margaret occasionally in the car mirror as she sat in the back, but I could feel her eyes on the back of my neck telling me that she did not need to be reminded. I excused myself mentally by telling her, if she were telepathic, that the whole idea of subterfuge was alien to her, and that she ought to try to be tactful. I waited for something untoward to happen.

Margaret used an attitude that Delicia must have experienced many times before from the social women whose business it had been to attend her. "Tell me about yourself, dear. How are you able to get about, and to what schools did they send you?"

We were away, and the conversation rode on safe lines.

"I suppose your father's at work?"

"No, he isn't." Delicia showed a flash of spirit. "He's unemployed, and can't get work."

"Oh, that must be terrible, dear," Margaret said as though she had heard of that situation.

I reflected that at least Delicia could not make any mistake about not knowing she was Mr Wether's daughter. She acted that part quite perfectly.

I drove out on the main road to the road-house I had chosen while Margaret subjected Delicia to the social version of deep analysis. When we got out, she said, "Let me look after you, dear, now we are here."

I saw something else. No one, not even I, could tell whether Margaret was actually being kind, or if it were merely that she could not help being that way as a hostess. Confronted by waiters and a strange place, it was as natural as anything else to her that she was handling a girl who was outrageously dressed and a cripple. Some people have it, and Margaret had. The man at the door sensed it, and the head waiter got it at one glance.

Well, why had I married her? I could not remember. The astonishing fact was that, though it must have been in her somewhere, she had been uncertain in those days.

It was almost exactly twelve months since Margaret and I had been out to a restaurant together, and now she had Mr Wether's money to spend, and, so I had told her, more or less a blank cheque. There was no doubt that Margaret thrived on blank cheques. Perhaps not more than other people.

"Are you going to take your coat off, dear?" She watched Delicia undo it. One glance at the dress, and then, calmly, and not open to question, "No, you'd better keep your coat on." To the waiter, she said, "The young lady will take clear soup." About the cutlery, she who had been born to it, said, "Now let's see, just which is the right spoon?" Delicia looked at her at that. It was a little bit too much, and at one place at least they had taught her the right spoon.

I wondered whether to try it. I had the option. I could take them home, or drop Margaret. I was starting to notice how things were fitting in. By saying I did not know when the firm would want the car back after lunch, I had kept all options open. Margaret had begun to look bored. There was no more intimate contact between women than to go shopping together, especially if one got the benefit and the other held the purse strings.

"I have a problem, dear." I let Margaret see it was awkward. "The Society wants to buy Delicia some new clothes."

"I am not sure, Dalby, that I should not get back."

With a wife in Margaret's position, it was a computer thing, really.

"As you like. I just thought, since we had the car and could go to a town to take a look at the new things."

I thought about it later when I was parked in a no-waiting area outside a shop in the High Street of a nearby town. No woman had a sense of time in the first place.

I thought about reality. How real was real? I imagined Dobson, never mind Delicia, learning someday that Delicia was not his daughter. I thought of the absent mother of the family. Could either of them disprove it? How likely was likely? I made a new twist and established reality on a new plane. A traffic warden came up, and I said, "I'll drive round if you like, but my daughter's a cripple, and my wife has her in this shop." I watched him engage with the problem.

I was still there, talking to the warden, when they came out of the shop. The warden saw one reality with his own eyes, Margaret another, and Delicia a third. For a moment, I felt panic, like a juggler with too many balls in the air. "Oh, thank you," Margaret said to the warden. Delicia's eyes were far away, as though she were viewing some inexpressible delight. Hanging from the fingers of her hands which also grasped her crutches were numerous parcels. Margaret looked younger. With someone else, a Mr Wether, at the other end of the cheque, she had played the grand lady. I could have forecast.

Success? It made me a little frightened and humble. Was I serious? I saw vista lined with mirrors that reflected one another stretching away to the future. The mirrors had the fragility of the surface of a pond, and I drove home expecting someone to drop a stone that would destroy the reflections and cause chaos in a moment. I could not remember the drive later. I presumed I did not hit anything on the way, but I was thinking whether it were possible, even conceivable, to live like that in the future.

I drove straight to Dobson's cottage, to confront Margaret with Dobson. It had to hold, the structure I had created. I must either test it or break it.

"Oh, thank you," said Delicia. She looked at me with appeal. "You don't need ... my father ..." We were arriving.

I wondered what she thought would happen when Margaret met her father. I drew up at the cottage. Margaret was made of sterner stuff than that. I thought, for a fragile passing moment, that I did not know how stern.

"Don't thank me, child, thank the Society," Margaret said with a lie so rigid it was like an elephant in gum-boots. She got out when I did, and I thought now, if my experiment were to succeed, then this was it. I introduced her to Dobson, who had come to his gate, and I thought of the panic I had sometimes felt should she somehow see me there. Was it not better to be so much more in the open?

She had some of the parcels, and she said, "Now, Mr Dobson, we will bring these things in for your daughter." She was examining him, as I knew he must see, as though he were something on a fishmonger's plate, on a cold slab. I could

146

only watch it and wait, and see reality, like an invisible fluid, flow around and fill all the holes in my stories.

"You don't need ... please don't bother, Missus ..." Later, Dobson said my wife was "a lady". But at the time what was apparent was the anguish in his eye, that was obvious, too, to Margaret. She spotted in a moment that he was afraid that if she took one look in his house, she would see something she should not see. She moved forward, in a way that would have taken a better man than Dobson to stop her, and went on and in, and by some process no one knew, she was with Delicia and up in the bedroom.

I wondered, looking at Dobson, who would not meet my eye, if Delicia were suffering and feeling separated from me. Then I thought, who did I think I was? She was a girl, with an outfit of new clothes ... It was going to be that which she would remember once the day was over. Margaret came down and gave Dobson one look and said, "Good day, Mr Dobson." She got in the car, and did not answer when I said I would drop her near the High Street.

I waited for her to answer. I wondered what it would be. I had laid it all out, and I had no more aces to play; I had been as open with Margaret as I could be. I could see by the way she looked at the streets she did not see there was something. I remembered as I drove that she had been virtually house-bound and able to do nothing for months, and that one of the Kingsmans had once been a prison reformer. She had that light in her eyes.

"It is disgraceful," she declared when we neared the centre of the town. She did not appear to notice that I did not answer, but went on looking straight forward.

She said, "You must tell your Mr Wether that he must do something about it."

Even I was a little taken aback.

"I told you how it was. What exactly—?"

She told me exactly.

"You realize that if the man is not the father, Dalby, it is indecent that that girl should stay there."

I had to turn my head away. Success! I could not let her see I was weeping, I did not know quite why.

20

It was the money that worried me most.

I thought about it on the day, a week later, when I took Margaret on her own in the car to Penfolds. She did not know she was going to Penfolds. I was dry-mouthed.

I had not yet got enough money to buy the place, and I did not know how we would live when we were there. I was pushing the collection of money as fast as I dared, and I wondered if it were too fast. I was worried about that, because I had been nearly caught only three days before, yet it could not be too fast. It was not only that I wanted the money for the purchase, but people were starting to be warned, and I had a name in the press. I was engaged in a small way in a race against time, and even Margaret had remarked on it on one occasion. She had said, "I hope you don't carry sums of money with you when you go on Mr Wether's business, Dalby," and I had noticed she was reading a column in the paper. SNATCHER STRIKES AGAIN was the headline.

It was worrying because I knew that the sole reason for the success of my robberies was the element of surprise, and a man of my age could not expect to succeed by brute strength or by speed. I had been almost caught because I realized the need for a new economy of action and speed. It had been in the doorway of an insurance office, one of the kind in a building in the centre of a Georgian terrace, with offices on three floors.

I had taken the money when the man passed the doorway, and I staggered rather than felled him, but long enough, so that when he turned round he was faced with a closed door.

I knew my escape route and went off through the back, relying on the indifference and slowness of the people in the offices to the hammering and ringing, since in daytime that front door was always left open. I had been very nearly trapped. When I went to the back, to a door that I had previously used when exploring the building, I found it was locked. Amid the knocking and the sound of the continuing typing, I had to go back to a passageway store-room and look on the key rack. I was lucky. It was there, and was clearly marked, Toilet. I went out through the backs, and through an office on the far side again and into the next street. It had been a near thing, and it had told me that so far as getting the money went, I could not go any faster.

There was one way I could always get money, and a very large sum, and it was always in my mind, but even I knew it was madness, and had to rule it out for technical reasons. I did rule it out, and so far as I knew I always would, and I tried not to think of anything like that while we were riding to Penfolds.

If what I was doing happened—and I placed the chances at fifty-fifty—then I would get the money somehow, I was thinking, when Margaret said, "Where are we?"

"On our way to the sea," I said.

"So I see, but I don't understand what your employer wants, and why me?"

She spoke as though she were going to meet Mr Wether himself at the end of the journey, and she looked at the ridge of moorland that was actually the cliffs, as could be seen by the light behind it, on the skyline. I calculated the distance we had to go to the cliff-road and decided that though I had refused earlier, as one way to get her out, I could start to talk to her about it.

"I suppose this is his reply to what you asked me to tell him."

"What?"

"You did say to tell him that Delicia Dobson should not

remain where she was, or don't you remember?"

Margaret was silent, I gathered surprised that I had passed on her comments.

"She should not, but I see no need, Dalby, for you to tell him what I said."

"I saw no harm in telling him. He was praising you for what he had heard you had done for Delicia. It is convenient to blame you for what I think."

I guessed that Margaret would digest that statement a little. We came to the coast road. She looked at the first glimpse of the sea, and said:

"I was not aware that you had told him I had seen the girl and that man. Just what are we doing?"

I agreed with her and apologized. "I have found it isn't safe not to say exactly what I have done. I think he knows someone who is in touch with someone down the road. He trusts me, I believe, but not to infinity. Mr Wether checks up." I was waiting for Penfolds.

"Dalby, just where are we going? Will you answer my question."

"We're going to look at a house."

"A house? What kind of a house? And what has that got to do with other people?"

Uncle Kingsman had died, and there had been a letter from Mavis, uncertain as to details ("Uncle died yesterday at midnight") but clear that she hoped to inherit something of his fortune and that there was no hope for us. I did not like cousin Mavis. There was a bottle of her medicine among my shaving brushes in the bathroom that had been there for two years. But the death meant we were looking for houses, and not exactly a cottage.

I could see Penfolds, but I did not say so. I thought it best to stage-manage so that Margaret got the best view. I said, "I've just remembered, dear. Did you tell the McFarlanes?"

I felt her looking at me though I did not take my eyes from the road.

"I don't follow you, Dalby."

"About Uncle's death."

"Yes," she said meaningfully. "I told them."

I knew she had, because McFarlane had had some uncomfortable words with me about it. She had said Kingsman died one day, but he had seen another date in the obituary in the *Telegraph*. I had wished that Margaret would either be accurate or sufficiently vague in her lying. McFarlane had also noticed that we had not gone to the funeral, which had been made impossible by Mavis's delay in writing. But I believed it did not matter and would have a bad effect on Margaret's confidence in her story if I told her. I had no wish just then to worry her with those things.

"That is the house," I said, letting her feel a drama.

We came round a bend in the road, and into the best view.

"I don't think," Margaret said after a moment's inspection, "that you will find we can afford that." She spoke quite sharply.

I gave her a key.

Her ideas of the monetary value of almost everything else that could be bought were very uncertain, but on house and land values she was almost invariably dead right; and I had given her a very limited figure as our uppermost ceiling.

"With Mr Wether's compliments, and will you look at it," I said. I was busy with driving and our arrival.

"Dalby," said Margaret carefully, "I don't understand you."

I drove down the lane to the gate, got out and opened it, and then drove into the drive before I told her. It would sound better in the garden. I made her wait in the car.

"He wants you to take more interest in Delicia. In fact he wants you to have her live with you. If you do, you can have this at a cheap price." I looked at Margaret for a moment as I told her the prospect, smiled at her, and then waved a hand, with an air of being humorous and deprecating I hoped, at the house and the garden and the sea view. I was conscious of a shortness of breath, a constriction of breathing.

Heaven knew if I were handling this correctly. I looked quickly away. I had always thought that Margaret's replies, and her attitude to almost anything, could be forecast, and I had built my campaign on my belief that almost wholly, and certainly more than anyone else in the world, I understood her.

In a moment, by my forecast, Margaret would say, "Dalby! This is outrageous." and I would agree with her and laugh. Above all, I would agree with her. I would agree with her all along, and deprecate the property. And then later, when we were leaving, in one hour, two hours, or perhaps not until tomorrow, I would come back. I would say, "Well, I suppose..." or "I wonder...?" I would create a situation in which I would say, preferably indirectly and without using the plain words, that since my money was dependent on Mr Wether, what alternative had we?

Such was my campaign for Margaret, but only God, not I, knew if it would work, or if my artistic creation—for I saw now, suddenly, that it was no less—could transform life and three hopeless people and make one thing of beauty.

"Dalby," Margaret said, she was turning slowly, looking at the house, the garden and the view down into the sea-cove, "It is cruel for you to play with me in this way."

My mind went blank. I did not know what to say for a moment.

"Cruel?" Was it possible that, more than I understood her, she understood me?

Margaret looked at the house. We had remained in the car whilst in the drive, but now she got out. She opened her door and slipped out, and moved forward, her head changing position as she looked at the split-level, the terrace, and the picture window. I had to get out of my side and run round the car to join her.

"It is not right of you to show me a place like this," she said, "for a man who is irresponsible, who is making a point, who is only joking."

"I don't see why..." I was lost for an instant.

Margaret stood for a moment. Then she turned and looked back at the car. It seemed she was leaving. She moved sideways, and then to the house, key in her hand and to the front door. She stopped and looked at me. "Cruel," she said, "because you know very well it is too like. It is impossible, and I think you might respect our one-time dreams, Dalby, when you know it is what we always wanted."

Then she went in. I too moved, then I stopped, and stood still, and looked at the National Trust scenery again before I joined her. It was good scenery, intimate in its view of the beach, and it could not be built on.

I thought, like a picture in my mind again, of what I was trying to do. I wondered if I were too aware that Delicia needed Margaret. I meant "need", not "like", since it was only someone like Margaret who could form and build her, not merely teach and train her, but transform her, make her a person. Was I acting for Delicia, and forgetting my own wife? I looked at the garden and saw Delicia in a wheelchair. I did not think so. I was sincere in my belief that Margaret needed Delicia, a child who would not grow up, an object and a hazard, even someone who would infuriate her. It was out of respect for Margaret that I did what I did, just because she was too big, and had too much life and energy unspent, and unlike too many women of her kind could not bear a lap-dog, and needed a blank canvas to work on.

And myself? I was sardonic about myself, and with my head turned from the house I could smile a little grimly. It was not an accident that, bought with "Margaret's money", the house would be in her name, and hers to do what she liked with, I could only hope to take in paying guests if it came to that, if I were at some stage arrested. Maybe... But if I stayed free? For the next twenty or thirty years I would have enough to do to make it work, and admire my creation. A "purpose in life" was not there, pre-existent in nature, it had to be chosen and made, and I could not see any better.

Was it a bad dream? I had better satisfy myself, and I did, before I too went into the house and to Margaret.

She was standing where I expected to find her, in the bare empty living-room, by the window, with the view below her. I wondered if she had already seen the kitchen and bedrooms and what I mentally called "the girl's room", but I did not think it mattered.

I went in and stood by her. I told her, "He means it."

She looked at me, and it was her look that was outrageous. "How can he?"

"Think of his position. He can't acknowledge her. He does not have that kind of wife or position. How is he to remove her from Dobson? This is in effect his reply to you. For us, acting as philanthropists taking an interest in the girl; it is just possible, we might do."

Margaret looked at me steadily, and I had rarely seen, certainly not in physical love, such a glare from her dark eyes.

"With a man like that, do you think I could possibly lend myself to a thing of this kind; you, Dalby, who by now ought to know me?"

"Yes," I said.

The black glare continued.

"I am no fool, Margaret. This is something you could do. You in particular. You are the only person I know who could do it."

For a moment, I wondered if she had any respect. I knew she could have very little left for me. Then I saw she was visibly shaken.

"Can we meet him?" she said, and her lips curled as though she already knew the answer. "Will he face us; and have it out in the open?"

"No."

"And just why not?"

"He will meet me and not you. He has notions about women. If you so much as know who he is, he is dead certain that in five minutes or five months you will be talking about the whole thing to his wife."

I saw an expression cross Margaret's face, and I knew with certainty that I had got her right, that it was that kind of thing she had thought of when she said "out in the open". She suddenly left me, and went off to the kitchen. I felt, at the time, as though I were handling some complex operation with wires and electronics.

She called to me from the kitchen, "Really, Dalby, do you think it is practical? How could he work out all the details?" But I let her talk to herself and did not answer.

She knew as well as I did that the details could not be worked out in a shouted conversation, and it was the main point, the principle that had to be accepted, and only after that came the trouble with the details.

Again she called. "Why do you think the girl would come to us, and her father, as he thinks he is, give his consent if we asked him?"

I let her wander round the house, and I joined her eventually when she came back, in the bathroom.

I said, "This won't please you. You have a dislike for white tiles."

She ignored the tiles and looked at me. "Did you hear what I asked you?"

"Yes. When Wether put it to me, I thought it was possible. Between us, we might persuade them, but that is not possible until you have made up your own mind."

She stared at me, and I sat on the edge of the bath.

"You are throwing this on me, Dalby?"

"Yes. It is you who will have to deal with the girl if you have her. You have met her."

She looked out of the upper pane. Above the lower frosted glass, there was even a view from that window.

"I once thought I would give anything for a place like this," she said in a torn way.

"I know. Or I thought that you might."

"I mean anything!" She looked out at the empty countryside, as at her father's onetime acres. "Do you think I tell you everything that goes on in my mind? It's a thing that you don't know."

I was surprised. I had under-estimated the effect of the house itself, not only its style, but its position in the crown of a view, and her atavistic feeling.

I said, "There is no hurry. You have until another purchaser buys, but the question is, will you?"

Perhaps I was not surprised enough.

I knew the kind of house she liked, and her feelings for wide open country. It could be for me that she had repressed all her inner ambitions while we lived in the town, but in that case I could not be blamed for not knowing that side of her nature.

She turned to me, not like a girl, and not with that dizziness, that sometimes affects women when they look at a new house, but like a woman in command of herself, and perhaps, as she thought, even me.

She said, "Yes. We will do it."

I thought again about the money. I felt I was committed now to get it. It was a feeling such as I cannot describe. It was an agony, a pure joy of creation. It was a sensation, inexplicable and unknown to me before, which went through me like lightning.

21

I WAS CLUMSY, I was vain, I was foolish.

It was essential that Margaret feel that she was the one who persuaded Delicia. I thought about that on the way home.

It was urgent. It was urgent because Delicia must be persuaded to come. I must get all these essentials fixed before I could put down a deposit and start the house purchase. On the way back, Margaret was practical. She discussed the price, and the amount Wether was to give us and whether it could be arranged in legal form or only by a gentleman's agreement. She faced the actuality of major changes in her life, with misgiving but without regret.

She said, "I imagine the first thing will be to put Derrington Drive in the hands of the agents." She wore a look of calculation.

"We had better think about that," I said. "Don't forget that this depends on two other people, Delicia Dobson and her father." About the Drive, she was not sentimental.

She looked startled. She was thinking of her own life and her own plans. She had got rather quickly, I thought, to thinking beyond where the plan was contingency-dependent.

"I will deal with that, Dalby. I will make the girl see the advantages of coming to us. I do not believe Mr Dobson can stop her. Don't you try." She put her managing face on.

I did not deny her intention. For her whole future, for all of us, she had to feel that she was the prime mover with Delicia, who must be her girl, and her protégée, not a girl whom I had foisted on her.

"I will see if I can arrange it," I said. "Do you think it

is too soon, or do you think you will be able to make her the offer if I arrange a meeting next Tuesday?"

"Yes," she said. "How can she do otherwise than accept? All that will be necessary will be for you to arrange the car, and for us to explain what we intend, and bring her out here."

I was sceptical about whether it would be as easy as that. I thought that Margaret was thinking more about the house and its arrangements.

Dobson I felt fairly sure of. At worst, I knew he could be bought off with money. It was the amount of money he might demand, and extract if he chose to be stubborn, that worried me in his case. It would be a great help to us, and to how we could live at Penfolds, if we, and not he, got Delicia's Assistance, but I saw in advance that it would be a main point. We kept coming back to money.

About Delicia herself, I thought it was essential to prepare her for her meeting with Margaret. I could see a calamity if Margaret failed to observe that Delicia was a person, and took too much for granted, and tried to "persuade" her by steam-roller tactics. At times, I understood Margaret too well. I did not believe she had ever asked herself why both Stephanie and Nigel had left home so early.

It was awkward telling Margaret that Mr Wether wanted to see me on Sunday, and arranging for Delicia to come out in the car. It meant the usual subterfuges all round just when I had felt that we were getting everything straight, out in the open, even if it was, as I hoped, for the last time. I even dreamed that somehow, after we had got to Penfolds, I could kill off Mr Wether. It would be so ideal if, after we were there, he had a sudden heart attack or accident and died. I felt a sudden, intense dislike for him, and no longer felt glad when I used him. I had to talk at the Dobsons.

If only I did not have to use him every time I "went out on business", and he were firmly dead, then neither Margaret nor anyone else could demand to see him, and it would be only of me that they could ever ask questions. I saw it as a situation passionately to be desired, but I could not yet see how to work it.

"I will take Delicia out for the afternoon now," I told Dobson. "I have the car and a few hours to spare. But my wife wants her for the afternoon on Tuesday."

"All right," he said. But he looked suspicious, and knew something was going on. "You wait here, I'll go and tell her," he said, and left me at the foot of the stairs. I could hear them talking, without hearing what they said, for quite a long time in the bedroom.

What was he telling her? I saw that introducing Margaret, "my wife", into a pattern in which he thought I was a sex-starved man besotted by Delicia, had created a new situation. I had made things more respectable, and he might very well be telling Delicia that I was losing interest in her in one way, the one way that mattered, and pushing her off on to my wife for "good works".

I wanted to deny this to Delicia as soon as she came down and I got her in the car. I wanted to reassure her and tell her I loved her, or that everything there had been between us was still valid. Instead, as I drove out to Penfolds, I was silent. At first it was because I was thinking, and then I was silent by design. The way I had to act, I told myself, was deviously, and not for Delicia's feelings but for Delicia's own good. It was something I could not help. I was fifty, and that was the nature of love at my age.

"How do you like the new clothes that Margaret got for you?"

She brightened. "I'm wearing this, don't you see? Don't you like it?"

"Why, yes," I said. "It is one of your new things. It's quite nice. It fits you."

We drove down to the beach. We passed the house, but I did not comment on the way. It was when we were on the beach, and I had smiled at her and helped her from the car and given her the help she needed to get across the loose sand to the rocks, that I created the situation I needed.

It was Sunday, and although it was still very early in the season, there were a few people about in the cove. An elderly man passed us, walking along the beach, and we could hear children's voices far away on the headland in the moments of silence that came in the hiss of the waves on the shingle. I wondered what they would think of us if they saw us, probably a middle-aged man and his poor crippled daughter; but we lay on the sand in the shelter of the rocks, and it was a place we still had to ourselves by the rock pools of green crystal water.

"It's good of you to bring me so far," she said.

She had never said anything was "good of me" before. It had always been that I, as a lover, was asking something of her. "Delicia," I said, turning on my side to look at her and blowing hot and cold, "you should not say that. If there is anything I can do for you, ever, I will do it."

"Oh," she said, and I smiled at her.

I dug up a stone from the sand between us, and held it up to the light and invited her to look at its colours. I swore there might be diamonds in it, and when she laughed and looked sceptical, I grinned at her and said, "Well, amethysts. There are crystals in some of them sometimes, and some of them are valuable, really." It was the kind of thing we did, finding treasure on "her beach" as a game, and then I lay on my back and was silent.

"Delicia, I have made enough money," I said after a while, when the silence had lasted. I knew she was still playing with the stone, and I waited until she was still. "I think I will stop work."

She did not understand. Then she tried to treat it as part of the game. "I bet you wish you could," she said with her cynical young voice.

I turned so that she could see I was serious. "No, it's true.

161

Something has happened, too. Margaret has an uncle who has died, and he has left her some money."

She lay propped against a rock, looking at me, and through me at Margaret, as at beings in another world, separated from her by the fact that we, who did not need money, who already had everything they needed, were the kind who suddenly got it.

"Oh," she said. She realized something was happening. "What are you going to do?"

"We're going to buy a new house," I said. I made a motion with my hand. The house was visible from where we were. It was from there we had first seen it. "That house. We are going to live here."

She let the stone drop. She looked at me in some strange way, as though she wished I were joking, and that what I had said were not true. "You're not!"

"We are," I said, and I shook my head gravely.

"I don't believe you."

"You don't have to believe me, my darling." I turned away from her and lay on my back as though I had taken offence and moved away at her doubting. "It'll be there. You'll find out."

I did not look at her again. I pretended I had said what I had to say, and I lay there, and perhaps in a while I would be sleeping. It was a silence that lasted.

Her voice came to me through the steady soft sounds of sea surf. "I suppose..." I could imagine her moving her hands as she did, as though tied by the legs, expressing feelings that in another child of her age would have found an outlet in running and action. "I suppose, when you're here, you'll not be coming so often to see me?"

I let myself seem to think for a while. "We'll have a car," I said. "It will only be a small one, not like the firm's car, but I don't see why not. Of course I'll continue to see you." I let myself continue to think. "Bringing you here may be difficult. There will be four legs to the journey."

I was silent again then. I had brought a book with me, and after a while I read it. I let her catch me looking over it at her as though I would like to take her in my arms and kiss her. But then, soon afterwards, I said, "Come on. We haven't so long here this afternoon. We had better pack up and go home."

We got into the car, which was quite a business, with all the things that we brought to the beach, of which we were beginning to have quite a collection. I drove up the lane. We had to pass the house on the way, and I saw her looking out of the window.

"Is that the house? The one you're going to come to?"

"Yes, it's beautiful," I attended to my driving. "You ought to see it." But I did not offer to show it to her. I felt sad and deceitful. I felt anguished, in fact, to play on Delicia. I let her see something then, when we were part-way home, and before we got too near to Lockley.

"Delicia," I said as though I were asking something of her, and not a free agent, "why aren't you more calculating?" I let her hear I spoke with feeling. "Why don't you think of your own interests a little more? No one else will, if you don't."

She looked shocked, even a little frightened. "I don't know what you mean."

"Like when you met Margaret," I said. "Don't you understand? Margaret is quite a rich woman now. She could do so much for you, almost anything. But I shouldn't say this. I'm her husband, and it's your life."

Delicia took a little time to work it out.

She got it suddenly. "You want me to make up to Margaret?"

"Not for me," I said hastily. "I shouldn't have said anything. For heaven's sake don't tell her. Don't tell her we've been out today. Forget it. Forget it, love. Don't remember I said anything."

I drove her home, and before I left, I said, "I'll see you."

I looked genuinely wistfully at her. "I'll see you when I come to take you out with Margaret on Tuesday."

On the Tuesday I drove them not to the same road-house, but to a quieter restaurant in the country. I discovered I had work to do. I would have to leave them. I hoped they would not be bored. I would be back for them later. I nodded to Delicia before I left as though she and I had an agreement.

When I came back with the car and they were in, Margaret announced to me, "Delicia's coming to live with us, Dalby." I turned. They were both in the back seat. I saw Delicia looking at me, a little frightened and anxious.

"Oh, darlings!" I did not have to pretend to be covered in emotion. I was moved. I saw Delicia's look blaming me for having left her to make the decision alone, but I had a strange feeling that humanity was good, and a reward and a warmth because she loved me a little.

'I'll have to ask Daddy." Mutely, her eyes asked me had she done the right thing. "He's ... I don't know what he will say ..." She was in a state of confusion.

"He will say you are a lucky girl," I said, and did everything to maintain her confidence as we drove back to the cottage.

I knew I could not leave it to chance with Dobson. I already felt that he would be bloody-minded. As we arrived down the lane, I blew the horn and said to Margaret, "Will you take Delicia in?" Dobson came to the gate in his disgruntled and slow-moving way, and I called to him and gestured. "Can you come here? There's something I want to show you in the car. Just a minute."

I got him to get into the front seat, and as the others went to the gate, I abducted him and drove off, stopping a hundred yards down the road. The women could think there was something wrong with the car. We just sat there.

"Margaret wants to adopt Delicia." I came out with it and

164

told him. "To care for her that is. Delicia is old enough to live where she likes."

He looked out through the windscreen and showed no emotion. I might have been talking about a strike at the works or some natural disaster.

"I thought there was something."

"We want your permission."

His face did not tense. I thought it was impossible for Dobson to tense. He seemed to go inwards and become several levels more sullen. He took his time about speaking, then said, "You can't have it." He knew I could not do it if he made a fuss.

He was the man who had been prepared to give Delicia away if I were a disreputable seducer who would pay him.

"How much do you want?"

His eyes shifted. He would not admit it was money. "I'll get old," he said as though that were unique to him and some catastrophe he could not face. "I'll be alone in my old age. Besides, how will I live, I need her. I need her Assistance." He looked ahead. He looked out of the car. He looked across the street. He looked anywhere except at me. What use would it be to tell him that it was at himself he was not looking?

"Oh, Dobson." I said.

"Yerse," he said, "but that's the way that it is." And he sat there, keeping still now, but looking ahead blindly.

What use was it, I thought? I saw. Was it his fault or mine that we were beyond the limits of reason? Would it have done any good if I had left him to Margaret? She would have pointed out the advantages to Delicia.

"All right," I said.

I could have told him that it was my intention to say that Mr Wether was going to make it a condition that Delicia should inherit Penfolds. I could have promised him the moon.

"Suppose we keep and look after Delicia, and you draw her Assistance."

"I want compensation." He meant that I would have to buy Delicia.

I too looked out at the road. The price had gone up because Margaret was "a lady".

"I'll give you a hundred."

"No."

"I'll give you a hundred in cash, in pound notes. Look! I'll double it. I'll give you two hundred."

"I want five hundred."

"You're mad."

We argued. We argued too long, while the others were waiting. I was actually frightened. I did not have the money. It was to be got "somehow". It was like seeing a vision and putting out a hand, but at every move it got farther.

"Two-fifty."

"Three hundred."

We solemnly shook hands and settled.

22

I DO NOT know how I can express, or if I can express, what I felt in this period. I speak of "a vision". It was a dream. It was pie-in-the-sky, I knew it. At times I would wake up. I would look out ahead at the world with an expression that I felt was all too like Dobson's. I was chasing a rainbow.

But a rainbow that could be caught? A vision that could be turned into the substance of flesh? I felt fear. It would be snatched away from me. Worse, it would never have substance. What was it? What was I contemplating? A beautiful life for myself and my wife and my mistress? Such things, in the world that we lived in, required money. Plenty of money. Not a background in which I had to beat down Dobson by a hundred, then quibble about fifty. And I knew I could get it. Or did I?

I felt a dread amounting to panic as I came to my main crime. How incredible that a dream such as I beheld should be dependent on money. Had I forgotten all I knew, all I had learned about the world over the years, having been in it for fifty? But my dream was only the picture the artist was going to paint, the book the writer was going to write, the symphony that was not yet composed; it was all in the mind's eye.

It was technically impossible, the crime that would give it some substance. In some way, it was not only or just that. It had something to do with my morals. It had to do with the impersonality of crimes. It was as though some crimes were vicious, and inspired by hatred, and some crimes were "pure" ones. It was like the time when I was a burglar who stole money from houses. It seemed then that I committed vicious small actions, though I was sure that they were not. I would take jewels from a dressing-table, and, since I could make no safe attempt to sell them, I would wrap them and flush them one by one down the toilet. Since I drew no benefit, it merely looked like a vindictive action. It was not. My object was to steal money only, and my action was necessary to create a confusion in the minds of the police. The jewelry was worth more than the money I took, and I had to make them think that the crime was that of a jewel-thief, so that they would set out to catch one. The action was "pure" in the sense that I had no will or intention of malice. But I could feel neither that purity nor anything else about my last crime, except a fear that set my skull crawling.

It looked and it felt so much like an act of vengeance against my one-time employers. It was in vain that I told myself that I needed a sum of something like £20,000 if we were to live peacefully at Penfolds, and I could think of nowhere else, nowhere else at all, where I could gain access to such a sum in one place.

The crime was technically impossible because, if I robbed the safe on the river flats at the Lee and Lawson factory, the police would ask for a list of past employees; they would ask who knew the combination of the safe, where the keys were kept, and who knew the burglar alarms in detail. They would ask who knew about the wages procedure, that they were there, made up on Thursdays for distribution on Fridays, and that the apparently dull ingots at the back of the safe were platinum and molybdenum alloys, and who knew enough about the trade to dispose of such things if they got them. They would come up with my name on all counts. I would be the victim.

If there was one person in the whole of England who could not burgle Lee and Lawson's factory successfully, it was me. And that was why, although I had known of the possiblity all along, I had pushed the whole idea right to the back of my mind, and had deliberately not thought about it. It was madness. There was the fact that the combination of the second lock on the safe was known, up to the time I left, by only three people.

It was not only that. It was the sum and the amount that was involved, and the fact that, if successful, I could retire to Penfolds and commit no more crimes. I would have enough cash from the wages for a start to cover the cost of the house and a car and to pay all expenses; and the metals, properly handled, and not sold at all for a year or two, and then in small amounts and with the utmost discretion, would last me a lifetime at my age. Mr Wether could be killed off.

The very fact that it was to be a "last crime" gave me a ridiculous, and irrational and fated, "so-near-and-yet-so-far" feeling. It was not logical. It was just the feeling, perhaps a carry-over from a belief in a righteous God in my childhood and from conformity all my adult life, that if there were any vengeance, and any blow of fate to fall on me, it had to be this time. It was there, and it was dreadfully final. But I decided to do it.

23

I WILL TRY to tell exactly what happened that April and May, when we were planning our move to our new house. I distrust explanations. I only know how it went wrong.

McFarlane came into it. That was one thing. Another was that I told Margaret that we must have a car for all the to-ing and fro-ing between Derrington Drive and Delicia and Penfolds. We had not got her "uncle's money" yet, but we must "borrow" it somehow. The last thing was that on fine afternoons I would go off, on Mr Wether's business, and spend time with a pair of binoculars lying hidden by gorse and heather on a hillside. I will take these things in order.

Margaret and I had never talked to the McFarlanes much. We had lived alongside them for twelve years, like other people in the Drive, but we had never got "close". It made a difference that I do not think is exceptional when we put the house in the hands of the agents and they put up a For Sale sign at our front gate, and we had to tell the McFarlanes we were moving. Margaret had to tell them where we were going, and that her expectations under her uncle's will were now firm. There was constant talk and asking about plans, and they learned more about us in weeks than they had learned in the twelve years.

I viewed these developments with apprehension, but I did not see how I could help them. I could not tell Margaret to avoid the McFarlanes, for I could not do so myself. I have mentioned how McFarlane stopped me and asked me on what day Uncle died, and to comment that we had not gone to the funeral. Now, when I had to tidy up the garden for the sale of the house, he stood constantly on the other side of the hedge either watching or talking.

One incident was typical. He had his *Telegraph* under his arm, the same paper in which he had seen the Kingsman obituary, and he watched me weeding the flower bed for quite some time. He spoke out of the blue.

"Your wife's uncle left his money to the Cancer Research Foundation," he said casually, "so it says here."

I went on weeding for a while, and then looked up at him. I smiled. It seemed to me natural. I imagined that everyone of fifty and over always smiled when nonplussed.

"Is that what that paper says?"

"Yes. Would you like to see it?"

"No. You should stick to *The Times*. The *Telegraph* is too full of Tory opinions."

"I see," he said, smiling, but looking a bit nettled.

I did not think it was wise to leave it like that. I wondered what Margaret had said when it had been put to her, as I did not doubt it had, by Mary McFarlane, and I thought I must try to remember to ask her.

"Does it tell you who in the family got the pre-death-duty hand-outs?" I applied the smooth ointment.

"The what?"

"The old man was a financier. You don't think he left it for probate and a will? Does your *Telegraph* tell you such people are not bound by the law?"

"They collect death duties if you make a gift within even seven years of your death." I was right he was nettled.

"The Cancer Foundation is a charity, and maybe they have a loophole. But he knew he was going to die for a long time, like other people with cancer."

He looked at me for a minute, and then went off to tell his wife about it. I thought a lot about McFarlane. Almost loving. He was between seventy and eighty, with a weak heart, liable to die at any time, no possible motive for crime, and, I felt sure, a police record that could only consist of a blank card.

I called him back. "I say! Do you mind if I borrow your garden shears? I seem to have damaged mine, and I want to have a go at the hedges."

He gave me another of his looks, went off to his garage, and came back with the shears, which I took by the blades, not the handles.

"Thank you," I said, and went off to my own garage with them.

I had never tried to take a fingerprint off anything before, but I tried then. The garden shears were good, he had used them with garden-grimed hands, but I could see it was a difficult technical process. I left the shears where they were, propped up on the bench since it was fortunately lunchtime, and slipped down in the afternoon to the Lockley branch of Halfords. I bought some French chalk, a roll of Scotch tape, of the kind that takes fingerprints very well when you touch it, and a small kit of cold-setting plastic and filler to make things. It would not be impossible, I thought, when I brought the items back. I had heard that in some of the less reputable police forces in the world they sometimes did it. The impossible was the start of the process.

What I made with the plastic was a finger. It was not very difficult, and anyone can try it. After that I clipped hedges. I worked up a sweat, and then went in and tried my plastic finger. I rubbed it on my face and then on a clean sheet of paper, and then tried it on glass. It was a matter of using the right amount of sweat and the right pressure when making the transfer. I would need to practise. I returned McFarlane's garden shears to him, and told him I had been down to Halfords to get a new bolt for mine, and they now worked. I had no intention of involving McFarlane in any crime. His fingerprints were just prints that were not mine but that I could use where the police might expect to find mine. It was a matter of choosing someone of whom the police would have no record. I did not think of him as a victim.

By now, I was creating a new reality. I liked to get it

clear and intact down to the very small details. I spent time wondering how, if I had the money, in pound notes and fivers say, I would pay for the house. I could not exactly walk in with the money. But there were the out-of-town banks, where I had in some places opened small accounts while standing in the queues and waiting for victims. Business accounts for ready money. I could use those accounts more, and shift sums into the post office Giro. Eventually, Margaret would receive a cheque. Margaret? It would be our joint account that would receive the cheque, though it would for a while be hers. I had to think carefully how to keep control. I left the garage where I had conducted my experiments and went in.

I told Margaret about the will and the report in the *Telegraph*, and expressed doubts about McFarlane's understanding of death duties levied on gifts made before death. The law was complex, and we had better look it up and get it quite right, and I noticed she looked dismayed and taken-aback for a while. She said she would have another talk with him or Mary McFarlane, though in fact I wished she would leave it to me. I could not argue with her as I had something else to tell her.

"We need a car."

"A car?"

She saw our need of one, but did not see how we could get one until we officially had the money. "You have expectations," I said. "I am going to borrow on your expectations."

"You can't do that."

"I can."

I did not only intend to borrow on her expectations. I wanted it well established that she was going to get the money before anything else happened, so that by the time there was cash in our account it would be stale news that would not be connected with anything else that was going on. I took the opportunity of a talk with the bank manager to mention the prospects, but knew better than to ask him for credit. Instead, I went to Fred Talbot, who, for all our one-time close business acquaintance, I had only seen once since I was unemployed, when he had refused me a job. It was no use having misgivings, for I knew I could not afford them, and I went to his office without appointment and sat there watching his secretary until there was a gap in his work and I could be shown in.

There was a lot of talk about "And how are things with you?" and "I'm fine." We were both stalling. He knew I wanted something, interrupting him in the middle of a busy morning, but he did not know what. I think he was relieved when I told him.

"Relax, Fred, I'm not here to ask you for a job or to tie myself round your neck for life. Things have changed, and my wife's coming into some money." I told him the story. "I want to borrow two hundred, just on my say-so, and I shan't be a bit worried or put-out if you turn me down." I smiled at him. "I'm a little past that, and as a matter of fact I'm getting a little kick out of it, going round to rediscover who my friends are."

It was true, in a way. I did get a certain enjoyment from putting him on the spot. I could be lying, but then again I might not, and if I was going to have money again, and perhaps sums to invest, that was not the kind of thing that anyone could afford to neglect in Lockley.

He recovered quickly, I admired him for that. "Are you offering me any security?" He was already reaching for his cheque-book.

"No." I said: "It's fine weather we're having."

I knew I was pushing my luck hard at that time.

I had never had a personal loan from anyone before, and, as I told McFarlane when I came home with a very small and old car, I was pleased to find I could do it.

McFarlane and Belfont came into my drive to look at the car when I stood there polishing it, and there was some talk about whether I should leave it to a museum and whether it ran on coal and water. Meanwhile I could see the women of Derrington Drive walking up and down and telling one another, "He is spending her money before she has even got it."

"I will tell Talbot I will take over your loan," Belfont said. "You would have done better to come to me." He was thinking of an easy fifty pounds in two months.

"You won't. He'll do anything for the church charity. He'll keep it." I watched Margaret looking out of the window.

The car and the For Sale sign on the house had done the trick, and I believed that Margaret's money was well-established by then, more than anything she said to the McFarlanes.

I went on three afternoons, with an interval for a wet day, on car-testing drives in the country. What I did on my afternoon drives was to go to a hillside I knew and lie there and watch quarrymen working through my binoculars. I did nothing for two days after that. On the night of the next day I went out on the bicycle, telling Margaret that there was something wrong with the lights of the car. It was a very bad night, with rain and driving mist and a gale, and I came home at two in the morning drenched and muddy. I told Margaret that I had fallen off the bicycle, and I would no longer use it. I had a cut on my hand, and she was alarmed at my state and said I looked as though I had been lying or rolling in mud and would need some new clothes.

"I did. I fell in the mud, and there was barbed wire I did not expect, too," I said. She asked me where my outer clothes were, and I said they were too bad, and I had left them in the garage. I made an excuse and went out and emptied the pockets and the results in the garage pit. It would have been like her to go and try to salvage my overcoat, and the result could have been disastrous, since she would not have discovered the substances like plasticine rolls in the pockets without trying to do something with them. She might have put them in the fire, and though I knew from wartime that we might have survived, I still held my breath for a few days whenever there was a loud noise in the vicinity of our garage.

I knew it was necessary to think of things soberly and carefully.

The local newspaper published an account of a break-in at a quarry. It was by two men, apparently, and the explosives store had been broken open. Footprints had been found in the mud and on the floor of the explosives shed. It was possibly from them that the picture of the two men had been built up, for one was described as large, wearing workman's army-type boots, and the other a small man. A police inspector said that the police had leads to work on, and the IRA were not suspected. It was specific and detailed.

I thought the account was fairly accurate. No IRA group would have taken only fifteen pounds of explosives, they would have taken whole cases. No mention was made of fingerprints having been found, and I wondered if that was as well, and whether the police had any possible means by which they could be traced to McFarlane. I went and brushed my garage floor in case anyone might discover where I had been experimenting with loadings on boot-soles.

I let the first Thursday go past without making any approach to Lee and Lawson's. I had intended it to be that week, if only because there was too much incriminating evidence in my garage, but I did not feel up to it after the episode in the quarry. I had strained myself, and I had to wait for my hand to heal while the showers and sunshine of April turned to a dull west-country May. It must have been because of the IRA that they made the explosives shed so hard to get into, and I could only sweat it out waiting.

Because of the anguish and foreboding I felt, until the next Thursday came round, I thought the worst part was waiting. By the afternoon of that Thursday, I knew that it was not.

"I am going to see Mr Wether early tonight, and I am

going in the car," I told Margaret. "We are going to work out the details of the agreement on the house and it may go on all night." She had almost started 'phoning the police and the hospitals when I had been late on the previous occasion.

I felt terrible, yet elated. I had worked out every possible angle, yet something must go wrong. It was a sensation unreasoning and violent, yet I knew it. I had not even felt like that about the quarry, and that, so soon in the past, was already a nightmare. So, I imagined, must all great artists approach their *magnum opus*.

Alternatively, for sheer stupidity and blindness, I had the same ancestry as Dobson.

I drove the car down to the river flats at four in the afternoon, far too early. I felt sick. I drove into the disused yard of one of Lawson's old Nissen huts. I parked the car and stacked timber against it. It was a dull afternoon. I went to a corner of the yard, and I found that I was sick. I had temperament. I remember looking at the place where I had been sick and wondering if the police laboratory could find out who someone was from the contents of his stomach. We had had rissoles for lunch. I fixed the yard door. I had had to climb over the wall to get into the yard in the first place. I left the gate on the latch.

At five o'clock precisely, I began to walk along the road by the tall wall of the factory. There was damp in the air. I had an aching and wide-open feeling. The works closed at five-fifteen, and by then the men and women would pour out in the street and start to flood in the opposite direction.

Lawson's ran three vans on a regular shuttle between goods yard and factory. I had had trouble with drivers. They came back at five-ten, irrespective, to be too late for re-loading. I came nearer to the gate. It was the main entry to the factory complex, and it was a matter of timing. I thought this would be it, I would be caught in the first place. When a van came up and turned in at the gate, I walked in beside it. It was easy. I had always thought it could be done, despite the watch that was kept from the timekeeper's window, and now I could prove it.

As I went through, I had an awful vision of what would happen if I were caught. Explanations, no doubt. But if I were searched? I could not think they would search me. Dalby Pearson, ex-technical manager coming back. With gelignite in his pockets.

As soon as I was inside the gate, I had to speed up to keep abreast of the van. I slipped into the paint store. It was frightening, it was anguish, it was all the things I expected it to be when crime became personal. There could have been someone in the paint-store. There should not, but there might be. Then everything would be all up. I would be confronted by one of my own ex-employees. At five-twelve they had gone off to wash. To wash after working was something all true Lockley workmen always did in the firm's time. It was more risk for me than an ordinary burglar, but I slipped in the shadowed back of the paint-store, away out of the light of the windows, behind shelving and someone's thermos and paint kegs.

When I was in, I realized someone would come for the thermos. It seemed impossible they would not see me. They came in, got the thermos, looked around the store in the far direction, and went out and locked up. I did not feel bright. I felt my luck ought to run out at any moment.

I spent five hours in the paint store. It was mostly dark. I could not remember spending five hours doing nothing and just staying in one place, locked in. The smell of turpentine and paint gave an extra solidity to darkness. I was practising, I thought. I was getting some intimation of what it would be like to spend not five hours but five years in a police cell in prison. They were not pleasant reflections.

After five hours I dared to start minor movements. I dared to switch on my torch, heavily shielded, and find out where I was. I made entertainment. I began to take out some of the mass of stuff in my pockets. I even had some round my waist.

I had not dared to take it all out in the dark in case I should lose it. Now I could practise what I had also done in that impossibly inaccessible explosives store in the quarry. I could make nice patterns in the dust on the floor with my portable boot-soles.

It surprised me. I felt awed. Why did not other burglars take elementary precautions like sticking adhesive soles to their shoes that were two sizes too small? Was I a genius, or was I following some unadvertised common route to disaster? While I made the footprints of my big quarryman, and left McFarlane's fingerprint on sticky blobs of paint and transferred one really beautiful one in paint to the window, I walked around in my own shoes. I had bought the adhesive soles in Woolworth's.

After all, my two burglars had to break out through that window. They had gained access as I had, and they would do everything that I did. Only they left their traces. It seemed almost a lawful undertaking. It was moral. I had a fanatical desire to create confusion in the minds of policemen. With gloved hands but a print from McFarlane, I used the jemmy the storeman used for paint kegs to break open the window.

I was sobered by the night air of the cold factory yard and the fact that the night watchman, an ex-policeman, would be out there somewhere and waiting. Even if he used to have his midnight supper at just that time, I could not be sure he would still do so. Dropping down from the window in darkness, I still had to use my heels to get the right pressure to make heavier prints with the big soles.

After crossing the yard in the shadows, I could have got into the office-block section through the small Gents' lavatory window. I dare not use it because it would show inside knowledge. My system of taking two burglars with me had some limitations. I had to choose an ordinary window in shadow, and since it was burglar-alarmed even on the side that faced the yard, a fact that my cracksmen might guess, I had to work there in the protection of shadow, which I would not have had in the street, and go round removing putty and sprigs and take a pane of the glass out.

It was desperate and frightening work, and I felt lonely at that time. I saw the light of the watchman cross the yard once, and just crouched there. Where was he going at that time? He went and came back to the timekeeper's hut from the Gents in the yard that the men used.

I was in. I was getting tired now, and for some reason depressed. It was just lack of food and the hour. I had the business with the boot-soles. There was a polished floor inside that gleamed in the dark, and this was the main point of entry. I had found a piece of material from an old jacket in the quarry. It would have quarry-rock particles and would come from a man who worked in the quarry. I thought bitterly of forensic and experts. I caught the cloth on a remaining sprig of the window and left them some threads there.

All this was too easy. It was not when I went through the silent interior to Accounts, into the chief accountant's office, a place that I used to know, where the safe was. For a while in the dark, listening to the silence I was going to disturb, I just stood there.

I had to get the key to the outer cupboard door of the safe first. It was in the second drawer down in the chief accountant's desk, and I broke all the drawers. When I saw the dull gleam of the safe, I wondered if they had changed the combination of the safe-lock. I had never done it in the dark. I took out the money and the things that I, as the technical man, used to keep there, with some quite small ingots. The money was made up in wage packets. I packed them in stationery cartons. I listened and looked out of the window.

It was serious, the next part. I knew I would have to use my intellect now, if I had one. It was no use standing. I had to get working. I wished I had more information.

I believed, from what I had seen on police shows on television, where they have a technical adviser to put the public right on such points, that the way to drill safes was to drill a small hole and feed in the explosives. It seemed logical. The explosion had to be inside, so that the safe door would be blown outwards. I dearly wished that Lee and Lawson's safe was the kind that would have made it easy by having a keyhole. I had to set to work with a hand-drill. I had thought about it, and must have gone over it a hundred times in my mind in the planning, but had decided that I did not dare risk the noise of putting on power at the mains. It would have been so much quicker if I could have used even the small kind of power tool. I got down to it, working mostly by touch, and remembered all I knew about metal-cutting as I laid out my drill bits. Before long I was sweating.

One small hole was all that was needed. It was not necessary for me, but that hole had to be there when the police examined the safe later. They make safes of a metal that is designed to make it difficult to make holes in. I had never realized how much there was to it before. It took an hour, and twice during that hour I had decided that I was not going to get through and that there was nothing to do but give up. I broke the drills three times. All I could think of was that the safe had to be blown. The police must never start even asking who knew the combination. And then at last I had to work delicately, being careful not to break the bit in the hole as I felt it start to go through.

If I had been a genuine cracksman, I would have had to roll out the gelignite into long thin strips between the palms of my hands and feed it in through the hole. At least I did not have to try that, but could put the explosives in by opening the safe door. I stopped and sat for a moment in the dark before I did it. Everything had to look to the police like a straight safe-blowing job. When a safe was blown, the money was inside it, and there would be bound to be scorched notes. I took some of the money and put it inside to be charred and be found there. I dropped some money on the floor, where it would be left by thieves who were in more of a hurry, and probably, I guessed, if it were conceivable, even more scared than I was. Then I packed the drill-hole with explosive and taped the detonator against it and laid out the fuse. The time had come when I had done all I could and could hope that the police would not even ask who knew the combination of the safe. I had to light my fuse and get out.

I used a long fuse and looked around with my torch to see that I had left everything in order. I overturned a chair and made everything look as though two people had been there who had left in a hurry. I wanted to get out and run, but if it was to be my last crime and my best it had to be right in all its details, and I was not finished yet. I went to the ground floor and looked cautiously out of a window that looked down on a side-street. The light there was poor and I was thankful and I looked out again after I had disconnected the burglar alarm and opened the window. I uncoiled my short rope of thin nylon. I started to feel sick again. There were a lot of risks in the next bit.

I went back and had the fatal "this is it" feeling again as I lit the fuse and made off with my parcel. I ran through the silent building to my window and looked out at the side-street. I attached the rope to the parcel and lowered it. I went down myself, by the rope. Every second counted though I had used a very long fuse. I used the rope, I dared not drop from the window. For I could have sprained my ankle, and, at that point, everything had to be just right.

The one big risk was that I might be seen by someone in the street when on my way to my car from the factory. Not at that time of night, I thought. But I went one way, and I saw someone moving. I went back and around. When I got to the yard and my car, I was late. I had the timber screening to shift from the car. I put my parcel in, between the front and back seats. Everything had to be right, and I put a rug over it.

I thought of the fuse that was burning. Fuses were not infallible, as I had seen at the quarry. I could only pray about that one. I never discovered a crime that could be done without risks. I counted the seconds. I needed ten minutes. I drove the car quietly from the yard. The yard door was open. The most difficult thing I did was to stop the car, get out, go back and close it.

I drove into the town in search of a policeman. I knew I would find one, unless I were extraordinarily unlucky, in the High Street. As I drove, I looked for the law in the dark shadows of alleys and doorways. It was the old car I was driving, and when I pulled out the choke, it would misfire. I had luck. I did not see a policeman before, but I found one in the High Street. The car backfired when I saw him. He was just standing in a doorway looking out at the night, and I slowed down, though I was moving slowly and irregularly already. I felt weak. I stopped just beyond him.

It felt like suicide. Perhaps they do, all the best things.

I had a clear picture of what I was doing and my timing, and maybe it was too clear. I smelled the night and the High Street of Lockley, and I thought of what would happen now, if the fuse went out, or if the detonator did not work, and there was no explosion.

I opened the car door and got out and came round the offside in the peaceful still night. There were no stars in the sky, but the shadows and street lights. I thought about God and the story I had prepared for policemen. I opened the bonnet and stood in High Street, far enough from Lawson's not to be "in the vicinity of the crime", and looked down at the engine. The policeman had to move. He had to come to see what I was doing, or I had to attract him. The air was quite chill now.

He came. I bent over the innards of the car, and he did what he had to do, which was to come over to watch me. I thought of the fuse making its last splutters at Lawsons' and of what would happen if the detonator did not detonate and the safe were found in the state I had left it. The policeman was bored.

"I think it's the carburetter," I said, and showed him. He had to take an interest in me. I was being too knowledgeable, and it was too obvious why I was late home and delayed. I became vaguer and pulled at the plug-leads. "At least that's what they told me." I was helpless and stood there.

He saw my uncertainty, and said, "Is this your car, sir?"

I said quickly, "Of course it is my car." I put a doubt in his mind, "I only recently bought it."

When I made to get into the car, moving away from him, he said, "Can I see your insurance and licence?"

I listened to the night, and asked him "What for?"

He moved to me. He was interested to smell my breath, though he made it not-obvious, and I let him. Politely, he said, "Do you mind, sir? I want to see your insurance and licence." I prayed "Please!" to some God or someone.

"My hands are dirty," I said, listening. It was time, and I knew it. I took my time, holding him there, while he did his routine work. I wanted to tell him a story I had laid on, but I did not get it all out.

He was covering my address on my licence with his hand when the night was disturbed. I had everything laid on, but I had been expecting it some little time when it happened. Checking up in the simplest way he could, he said, "What is your address, Mr Pearson?" There was a thud, followed by a tinkle of glass in the distance.

We both looked in the direction of the sound, and I asked him, "What is that?" He went on looking. He started to give me my licence back, but he still asked, "What is your address, Mr Pearson?" I told him, and took the documents back as he handed them to me, then he moved off.

"If I get the car started, I'll give you a lift," I called after him.

"You'd better get home, sir," he said. "It's probably some children."

I stood in High Street by the car, watching him go away. I heard sounds from the way he had gone. He seemed to be talking though there was no one else there, then I realized that what he was talking to must be the radio from his pocket. He stood for a while then he moved, and I was left alone with the street and the night sky.

At the time Lee and Lawson's was burgled it had already been known in the town for some time that I was getting money through my wife and was no longer pressed for finances. I had been out in my old car on that day and could call on a garage thirty miles away to give evidence that the car was giving trouble at the time that I called. By chance, and while passing through High Street, I was under observation at the exact time, not that the policeman would report that unless asked, but his testimony was there any time it was needed. I stood by the car, and looked down the street, then put the bonnet down and got in. I felt at the same time suddenly weak and exultant.

I went over it in my mind before I pushed the starter of the car. A crime was an edifice, or a construction like a car with I did not know how many components. If you put it together, part by part, from all the innumerable small pieces, could you expect it to go, and to work, when you first pressed the starter? I went over the things that I had done, thinking that there had to be a flaw somewhere. I must have forgotten some small thing, or made a flaw in assembly at some point, but I could see nothing wrong. I switched on the ignition and tried to drive home in the car and it spluttered and died.

It started the second time, when I kept calm and pressed the throttle wide open. There had to be a reason, and I had over-choked it. Before the engine ran evenly, I heard the twin horns of a police-car approaching. He was coming at high speed, and I went off down a side-street. In the police car they would be looking for who was in the vicinity of the crime, and that was different from the man on the beat who had met me without haste and before there was any crime to think of. Getting away with crime was not so much a matter of hard facts, it was more the psychology of people. I drove home and got out of the hunt in the night with great caution. When I arrived at my garage, I put the lights out and put the money in my private safe that I had dug in the wall of the pit, and replaced all the floorboards and drove the car over. It was still in the Drive, and I stood in the garden and looked at the quiet emptiness under the trees and the street lights. I was not even in a hurry to go into the house, for it was a beautiful mild night.

24

THE INGOTS, I thought. It was in my mind as I awoke, first thing in the morning. How many people knew where they were kept? They would get a line on me that way, and it was mixed up with my awareness of where I was, and my pillow. It did not last. A criminal has to have a disciplined mind, and for a while I just lay there, then I went back to sleeping.

There was always the remote chance. In fact Lee and Lawson's always had a stock of the more valuable metals and alloys, because it was part of their work on electrical contacts, and the safe was the one place to keep them. All the stock and electrical staff knew they were there. By talking to them, and knowing just what he wanted to know, any stranger could find out. When I really awoke it was late, and I just lay there looking at the light of the window and enjoying it, in an almost physical sensual way, as though I had found a new kind of pleasure. Getting up, when I chose to get up, I thought as much about the chances of arrest as a man does about the chances of being involved in a traffic accident, which is also a finite risk, when he wakes and gets up in the morning.

I spent some time looking out of the window when I got out of bed. Margaret was calling upstairs, but for a while I ignored her. I was seeing the Drive from a different angle from when I had looked at it the previous night, but it looked just the same. It would look just the same, and the town and the whole district, if someone had stolen the crown jewels overnight. It would all be the same in a hundred years, I thought, and all the events to which everyone attached so much importance would all be forgotten. You might as well do as much as you could for yourself, and keep a true sense of proportion.

Margaret went on calling to wake me, to ask if I were coming down and if I wanted any breakfast. I went to the door and told her yes. I thought of the physical shape I was in, and looked at myself in the mirror as though I had made an investment and had to take stock of what I had. I did not look bad. Sagging under the eyes and wrinkles, but the streaks in my hair could be distinguished. I had various aches and stiffnesses all over my body, and a blister on the palm of my hand. I knew many men of my age who would be in far worse shape after what I had done. I felt a young man at fifty.

I dressed and shaved before I went down. No one was going to see the effects of the previous night on me. Besides, I had a lot of things to do. They were not forced things, they were the things I wanted to do. I knew what the Western world meant by "freedom". It meant owning for yourself the means for what you wanted to do. There were words like "individual freedom". That meant it was possible to do what you wanted, if necessary, by over-riding other people.

They wanted that kind of freedom, I thought as I put on my jacket. It was their choice, Margaret's for example, who always voted for the party that had been supported by her father and his friends. It was not my choice, but I did not feel vindictive. It was merely that it was what they wanted, and they had bought it.

I had to be careful when I went down to Margaret. At the same time, I enjoyed it. All I had told her when I had come in late the previous night was that I had been successful. I had made an agreement with Mr Wether. I knew why she had been calling impatiently up the stairs to me. She wanted to know the terms of the agreement.

She had a good breakfast ready for me when I went down, though it was eleven o'clock in the morning. She sensed something these days, and had ever since I had shown her Penfolds. I cut more ice, I had more weight. Even with the loan Mr Wether was giving us, Penfolds was quite substantial. I might not be an utter failure after all. She could not help it, but it was a basic monied-class idea. How I got the money might be dubious, and it was very dubious in her eyes, but that faded into insignificance compared with the solid and indisputable fact, which I felt in some way shone out of me, that I had it. Monied people cannot take people without money seriously. They may be very nice, and have the best intentions, but they are not actually people. They cannot do things. They have not got what it takes.

"Dalby, what exactly were the terms of the agreement you came to?" Margaret asked me.

"More or less on the lines we envisaged," I said as I ate. I was aware that she was asking, not demanding. It was all to the good. She really wanted Penfolds. She must have been up two hours, and had waited patiently.

I could afford to be generous, and I told her the terms. At the same time, I was careful about them. They were my lever. They were what was going to make everything go as I intended. "I got the main thing," I said. "There must be no question of him taking over the house or otherwise dispossessing us. That applies if the girl becomes unreasonable or fractious or elopes with the jobbing gardener. We retain sole possession in all such cases." I told her all the good things.

"But he retains a lien upon the house?" Margaret said. She dearly wanted to get around that, and she knew all the slightly antiquated language of lawyers.

"I could hardly persuade him not to retain that, since he's putting up some money."

"It means that in case of dispute, he is final arbiter." She was standing in front of me, thinking hard and absorbing the details greedily, with her hand on the table.

"If you mean, can we just take Delicia Dobson in, then treat her badly, throw her out, or make life so unpleasant for her that she has to leave, then Yes. But it's up to us, isn't it? It's up to you. We can hardly say that it's going to be terribly difficult for us, since she has nowhere else to go, except back to her father." I looked up and smiled at Margaret. "I should think that if you put yourself out, you could reliably compete with her father."

She frowned. She accepted my tribute to her ability without thought, but she did not want to have to compete with anyone for the ownership of her house.

"What happens if things go wrong?"

"I thought of that, dear." I put it to her gently. "You remember, we discussed it, and I kept to what we discussed. If she does leave, or dies, or you and she reach the point where you are throwing things at one another in the kitchen, then what happens, quite simply, is that she leaves. If you think about it carefully, you'll see how far I got. Technically, this agreement can only be broken by one side, and that's us. We throw her out. From then on, we pay interest on the loan. It reverts to a mortgage."

Margaret looked into the distance. She said, "I don't like a mortgage."

I pretended to lose patience with her a little. "It's no worse than we have here."

I had not been making mistakes in my double association of Delicia leaving Penfolds with the fact of a mortgage. I hoped that, not always, but just that time, I was two moves ahead of Margaret. The mortgage was as I said, on the figures I had given her, no worse than we had at Derrington Drive. But it was a mortgage of a private kind, to Mr Wether. I had cards up my sleeve.

If it ever came to any question of Margaret throwing Delicia out, then, I would point out, Mr Wether was going to be angry, and Mr Wether was my employer. I would be liable to lose my connection with him. Without a job, how could we pay interest on the mortgage?

Despite the agreement, Margaret could only keep the

house as long as she kept Delicia, but that was unseen.

She accepted it as she had to, moving back to the stove. "What we must do is save, Dalby. I would like to be in a position so that at any time when we wish, we can pay off that mortgage."

"Naturally, that is what I think," I said, and finished my breakfast and got up. I did not tell her that, as soon as we got to Penfolds, Mr Wether was going to have a setback in business and cease to have a great deal of use for my services. I had thought of killing him off altogether, and I still thought of it sometimes, to create a truly static condition, but as I prepared to go out I had the mental opinion that, to keep Margaret in order, I had better keep him there in the background.

"Are you going out?"

"Yes."

"Will you be back to lunch?"

"My dear, no. Now we have got an agreement, I have a lot of things to do. Sometime today, I have to see the agents, the bank, and the lawyers." This was perfectly true. Now I had ten thousand in cash to introduce into the system, in the course of selling one house and buying another, I had to work on the principle of what-the-eye-does-not-see in some circular byways of economics.

I went out and spent that day in Lockley.

I had a number of things to consider carefully, including my position as a person who had come into money (or my wife had, which amounted to the same thing), among my former acquaintances and the people who also had money in Lockley. I had things to do, apart from visiting the bank in the morning and the agents and lawyers in the afternoon. For example, the first thing I did when I got into Lockley was to call in Smiths and buy a motoring magazine to read while I was waiting and lunching. I was considering the purchase of a new car, now the old one had served its purpose.

I was not oblivious of my earlier thoughts on the subject

of cars, and the atrocious waste of money on minor improvements of comfort and gadgets. It still applied, that anyone who spent an extra £300 on a car, never mind £3,000, was doing it at the expense of someone like Delicia, whose entire life they could change by the provision of something like a downstairs bathroom for an invalid trapped upstairs. It was merely that, as a man who now counted himself a success, I saw it a little differently. I was going to need a reliable car as a necessity when we were living at Penfolds. With inflation proceeding at the rate it was, the sooner my capital was in solid objects the better, and it would be false economy not to buy a car that would last five years or ten years.

I had also dressed carefully with the intention of having lunch at the Bull, and I did that. I saw Fred Talbot there, among the other business people who regularly had lunch in the dining-room, and in an unashamed way, and letting other people see me do it, I repaid him his loan. After all, I had two choices. One was to pretend I was still poor and to wait until the Lee and Lawson business had been forgotten before I announced my sudden acquisition of wealth. The other was to make it appear that the relative affluence had come about actually before the night of the robbery. I chose the latter course: "Hello, Fred. I've been looking for you for a week to give you this." Then I went on to sit at a table with a man called Blundle.

"I am glad to see you back with me," he said. We had commonly sat at the same table except on Thursdays. "We haven't seen you for some time."

"You weren't in last Thursday."

"No."

"As a matter of fact," I said, looking at him like an old friend confessing, "my wife has come into a little money, and I am a little shy about going around looking as though I am the one who is going to spend it."

He said, "Umph."

We ate. The same rule applied as I had noticed with

Margaret. How you got the money was a fact of the utmost insignificance to everyone, compared with the really important point that you were now alive again and able to spend it. In the middle of the meal, he said, "I wish my wife had an uncle."

An uncle? I had not said that to him. I saw. Fred Talbot had been talking. My wealth was established before the break-in. I need not have worried.

It was some time before I saw Delicia.

I needed to sort out my money in the garage first, and that meant waiting until Margaret went out, when I could count and stack and get rid of the pay-envelopes in the fire, and incidentally select some used, torn or possibly more identifiable notes, to put in a pile to give Dobson. I had not seen Delicia alone since the day on the beach when I had persuaded her to take advantage of Margaret. We had met two or three times since, but Margaret had been present, for I had other things on my mind and could not go to her for mere pleasure when I was under the nervous strain of working up to Lawson's. I had, therefore, not had a proper talk to her for a long time. I wondered how she would take my return.

I chose the evening, when I knew she would be upstairs and Dobson in the kitchen, and I completed my transaction with him first. After I had gone in, I put the money on the kitchen table for him, and asked for a receipt.

"I'm not going to give you no receipt. What's it for? You've got no right to ask it."

I was as careful as people with money are. "I want to make sure that you know you've had your compensation, and that you don't come asking me for more when that's gone."

The sight of all that money on his kitchen table was too much for him. It must have seemed that it would last him

193

for ever. As I expected, he went out to the pub right away.

"For God's sake, why do you want to take all that with you?" I asked, seeing what he was stuffing in his pocket. "What do you intend to do with the money, drink yourself to death?"

"It's no business of yours," he said.

It seemed quite possible that he did intend to drink himself to death, literally, as though that were the ultimate solution he had come to about life's problems. I went up to Delicia. I knew she had heard me come in, for I had called up to her.

I adopted my usual tactics of going up to her door, knocking, and walking straight in. It was an assumption of intimacy which somehow gave me disproportionate pleasure on that occasion, perhaps because it was something she could neither stop nor resist. It meant that no matter what action she was performing, she could not be sure that I might not see it, and now I felt sure she was wholly mine, whatever I did with her.

In fact, it was I who was surprised. She was sitting on her bed with her head in her hands and crying. I looked at her for a moment. Well, I thought, perhaps I had been treating her a little roughly. I had not had the time or ability to do otherwise while making it quite certain that she would come with us to Penfolds.

"Delicia, Delicia!" I said, and went to sit on the bed with her. She was dressed in one of her new garments, a thin slippery silk thing that was meant to be pretty, but that to me was determinately female, between a dressing-gown, night-dress and housecoat. I tried to put my arm around her, but she pulled away and buttoned another button of the coat.

"What is it?" I asked her. It took a little time to get her to talk at all, as I expected. After hearing me come in, she had allowed some resentment to rise to the surface and worked herself up into a state about something. When any girl did that, things had to progress more or less on set lines.

"Tell me," I said. "I can't do anything about it unless you

tell me, can I? Really, darling, tell me. You know me. I'll do anything to help you."

"You called me 'darling'," she said.

"But of course I called you 'darling'."

"You don't love me," she said.

Thinking back over our last two or three meetings, I could see she could have got that impression. They had not been exactly sexual, which was what she meant; they had been more like good works.

It was difficult to counter her statement without confusion. I did love her sexually. I had been aware from the start that I loved her sexually far too much, considering the difference in our ages. All the time I had been poor and uncertain, I had felt a constant guilt, both to her and to Margaret about it. Perhaps it had only been that which had prevented me taking matters further than they had gone. I understood what she meant well enough, but I was not sure that she did.

Even if she did mean it, I was not sure if she meant what she said. Most adult women, I knew, talked about sex and love as though they were two different things, and if you proved that by the one they meant the other, they took fright and withdrew. It was the language that was at fault, but it ended up as a confusion in their own minds, so that, sometimes, no matter what you did, it ended up with resentment.

We started a long, wrangling argument when she started to speak, most of which consisted of contradictions and illogical words and phrases that were often repeated. Infinite patience was required for that kind of thing, and I believed that from past experience I had it. It was terrible.

"You don't love me."

"But darling, I do."

"Don't call me darling."

"Sweetheart."

"You don't love me. You just want me to live with your wife."

The trouble was, as I knew, that it was all too easy to

195

argue with this kind of logic. I could say, "Why should I want you to live with us if I don't love you?" but that would miss the point, and it would miss it in a way that I knew was missing it, even though "love" in English, as anyone of my age knew, could mean almost anything.

"It will be horrible." She started on a new tack.

"My sweet, look at me. Listen to me. I won't let it be horrible."

"It will."

"Delicia, darling. You'll have everything you want, and we'll be together always."

"You only love your wife. You only love Margaret. You think I'm a young girl."

I began to be alarmed.

"You know you are a young girl, but don't you think I like that?"

"You don't love me."

"I do!"

I tried to touch her, to put my arm around her again, and she pulled away. If I could once get her to come into my arms it would be all right. The garment was slippery, and I began to suspect that she had nothing on beneath it. Was it accident that a girl always started this kind of thing whilst at the same time creating the maximum sexual effect. I tried to sit back and be deliberate.

"Don't you think I'm doing quite a lot for you, Delicia? Except that I love you, why should I want to look after you?"

"You want your wife to look after me."

"Delicia."

"It's true." We were both losing our tempers a little, and she turned around and faced me. "You wouldn't have me live with her if you loved me in that way."

I had gone far enough, and I said, "Exactly in what way?"

She looked at me with a tear-stained face, and said, "You know what I mean."

I put my hand out to her, and rested it on her shoulder,

while with the other I undid her buttons. I put my hand on her breast.

She looked at me with scorn. "That's all you do. That's all you've ever done." She began to weep again.

She came into my arms however, when I pulled her to me. I put my hand on her and slid it down to her thigh. I was very conscious that she was a cripple, and I knew that that, the unspoken thing, underlay very much of her tantrum. What I did was meant to comfort her, perhaps to convince her of something of which she would never be convinced until some young man infinitely more clumsy than I, if a young man would ever do it, chose to treat her as I did.

We were silent for some time, and then what I was doing roused me. It had happened before, and it was connected with her helplessness, her gratitude, and her desire which in her life could not find any outlet. Her father was definitely out for the night, and I began to ask myself what I was, a *voyeur*, or the male equivalent of those women who virtually and constantly enticed men and then drove them mad by being too timid.

I thought: Why not? On all previous occasions I had stopped at that point.

I began to undress. She soon discovered what I was doing. She made little cries. "Oh, Dalby! Oh, Dalby!"

I told myself I should not do it, a crippled girl, and a man over fifty. But I was partly undressed and I held her for a moment, thinking I would stop there. I always had before. What was different now? I found her pressing against me, inescapably sexual and shamelessly demanding. It was I who had brought her to that. I knew she would be nothing like that if I had not roused her. As she clung to me with her arms, she was breathing, "Oh, yes! Oh, yes," in my ear. It became vain, it became pointless, to tell myself that, with only a little stretch, she could be my grand-daughter. It was just a matter of the physical bodies, and actuality, the sexual truth that either was there or was not there; a sudden, overwhelming surge of desire on my part, a feeling that was almost literal blindness, and a thought that was unformed, but which, if it had been put into words, would have been, "You asked for it." I found I took off my remaining clothes, and I meant it.

She looked startled, and as though she might have second thoughts when she knew it was going to happen. It was too late. It was always too late when a girl got to that stage, but it was particularly too late for her. I just heard, more than thought, the rationalizations: she might never find anyone else; better me than no one in her life; it would ruin her confidence altogether if nothing happened now. They were all true, or they all seemed true, and there was nothing at all, suddenly absolutely nothing at all that I could think of against it, and it happened.

At least, because all mental opposition had departed, I was able to take it slowly, and make sure that it did happen. She saw it and felt it and knew it as something final, which was what I aimed for. It was done on the bed properly, with still daylight from the window, and she was left in no doubt as to whether she had or had not. I was proved right. It was physically difficult, and in doubt for a moment, and then she said, "Oh, we can!" and her voice went up in the scale but became fainter as her face echoed an anguish, and she said, "I can! Oh, I can!" with her eyes closed.

When I could, I rolled over on the bed and lay beside her. It was the same as with any lover, and what a girl most needs, the smile of reassurance, that it was right, that she had not done a wrong thing.

She was still for a while, lying on her back. Seeing her quite naked and full length, it was easy to convince myself that all girls' legs were like her legs. Anyway they were part of the fact that she was special, that she still was, what in some way she had been, my inspiration; more so when she struggled, rolled over, and buried her face in my shoulder, saying, "Oh, Dalby."

"There, there." I lay with her and stroked her. I had no care about her father, and did not mind how long I stayed, we would hear him in good time, and we had hours still before us.

I only thought, sometime during those hours, was that my dream? And was life different in success, and would anything else other than what we had done and what we would do often as each chance came at Penfolds, have been foolish, even wasteful, and what had to be called "sentimental"?

25

Life was ordinary, as it is for a successful man who is prudent, who pays for what he wants, who has business appointments, and can always invent them if he has not, and who goes to and fro by car.

I thought about my dream, my aspiration, in those days when, for a time, I went to and fro across Lockley. It was not one continuous piece of thought. It was put together, on different occasions. How had I got this dream, this objective of putting Delicia and Margaret together in the same house, not just any house, but a particular house, and living with them there, in some kind of beauty? It had been valid. I could see that. It still was valid. It still affected me. It was just that now, in the course of daily life—I had one house to sell and another to buy and there was plenty to do that I referred to as "business"—, and often in the car driving from one place to another, it was subject to a kind of analysis. I would think, It is this, It is that.

I was just the old selfish male, I thought. I was surprised I had not seen that before. The old dog-man with his tribe of females, and wanting to take them out with him to some place where they lived on the cliffs, where no other male could get at them.

Looking at a Lockley street, as I waited in a traffic jam in my car, I would think it was revolt. It was something I wanted to do, have two wives, just to spite people, because at that time, when I thought of it, I was at odds with Lockley, and feeling guilty besides.

Another time, coming out of an office and walking down the

High Street, I thought: For heaven's sake, any man wants a young girl if he can get her. All right, so she's very young, and a cripple, and you're too old. But what's all the fuss about? The heavens don't fall. Everyone has it in some way, only some aren't so lucky as to put it into practice, their own particular line of perversion.

It was as though I were trying these thoughts out. I was, after all, behaving like an ordinary better-class Lockley man, like a Derrington Drive man, who had quite legitimately come into some money when he needed it. Nothing exceptional about that. Before long, I almost believed it myself. When I thought in these ways, reducing my dream, it was as though I were trying to get away with something.

It was more than that. It took me a little time to puzzle out what I was doing, and why I had such thoughts. On another occasion I was walking out of my garden, and comparing it with others in Derrington Drive, when I thought: A power complex. That was all it was, my beautiful dream, with all its thoughts of fine art, and creating something in real life, not as others did, on canvas or paper. It had been at a time when I was powerless, and so I had been trying to convince myself that I was something special, that I had more power than other people.

I went on with thoughts of that kind while I was driving down the hill. In fact I had nowhere urgent to go, not even to Delicia's, on that day. Then I thought: Why do I think like this? I am not trying to get away with something, I am kidding myself. I am trying to get away *from* something.

I had no idea if other artists went through this stage, when they got near its completion, of denigrating their own creation. If they did, I thought, they would kill it. Their very success, if they were successful artists, would cut them off from the roots that gave them the desire in the first place. I could see plenty of attractions around me, pretty girls coming out in their summer clothes in Lockley, and new cars. It was easy to be distracted.

It could have been because I had obtained my money illegally. I was not quite what I seemed, after all. Walking down the High Street after I had parked the car with difficulty, I was still a fraud, and as I knew when I thought of it, a crook. It could be that that was why the cheapening and denigrating thoughts did not quite work. At times, I thought, Oh, what the hell, what am I doing this for? Do I have to take Delicia to Penfolds? That will be a right mess. But when I did think that, I did not quite accept it. The dream looked sometimes a little worn. It faded a little, like an old television, that worked in a dark room but was then put out in full daylight. At times it seemed ragged, and it sagged. It began to look weathered, and a bit intermittent.

But it held. It did not quite break. It lost its colours slightly, and its shape, and was washed-out.

26

THIS PERIOD LASTED several weeks. There were plenty of details to arrange and people to see, and perhaps because I could not arrange my mind easily, and had to accept that what I had put my mind to I must do, I still went ahead. I could not break out of my involvement.

Things happened, small things. They were sometimes difficult to define. It was not that the events in themselves looked important. They were the ordinary day-to-day affairs of house-moving. It was as though the details of ordinary life, that looked so ordinary and straightforward now, and yet which contained something that I was afraid to believe until it happened, were shot through with hard sharp sparks of anguish. I knew I was on a down-slope, but I did not know *what*.

I drove Margaret out to Penfolds to measure for curtains. It was all going and coming. We seemed to have only arrived and started when I had to say, "What time do we have to go back?"

"I am not going back in time to cook." Margaret was definite. "You'll have to make do with a cold dinner, Dalby."

The room was still empty except for two light chairs and a card table we had brought and that made it look emptier. There were more measurements to be taken. I looked at the room and could not believe, for some reason, that we would ever live there.

I looked at Margaret working. She had that flat, tireless energy of old women that makes them so much tougher at ages when men often get frailer. But she still did not seem to be happy. She too seemed as though she were working against some fatal knowledge: that what she worked for could not be. This was happening again.

She turned to me suddenly, harshly.

"How long will it take you, Dalby, to work off the mortgage?"

I wondered if it were connected with Delicia. I had been expecting it in a way, some kind of outpouring. It was unnatural the way that Margaret seemed to have accepted, almost without complaint, the need to have an alien, working-class girl in the house. I had sudden dire feelings about how it would be, when, if ever, we were there. That mortgage, as she called it, had to last for ever. The possibility that she might lose the house, if there were interest to be paid and I could not pay, was my trump card.

"You are harping on a bit about that, dear."

She said, "After the experience we have had of a mortgage!"

In the competent way any efficient businessman has, I turned it into something positive.

"You really like this place, don't you?"

Looking out of the window, Margaret gave me an unusually unequivocal and passionate, "Yes!"

"Why?"

I had no idea at that time that I was dealing with uncontrollable forces.

"Dalby, it suits me," she said in a flat voice.

I tried to see why. I believed I could in a way. To Margaret, our town life had always been second best. I had some idea that it was more than that. In offering her something like Penfolds after what life in Derrington Drive had become, I had probably gone further than was necessary to make her adopt my plan or any other. In the current language, there had been a certain amount of overkill. I saw it in that way.

I looked at the sea, thinking that with its perpetual motion and changing lights and colours, I could look at it always.

It was probably better to bring her down to earth a little, and maybe use her momentum.

"How is it going with the McFarlanes?" I asked. I was not unduly worried, but I felt I had to keep my eye on that situation. I thought it was neutral.

"Don't let's talk of that."

"Has he asked any more awkward questions?"

Margaret turned to me. I thought she was going to burst out with something. She seemed to have an obvious anger. I thought it was because of what I had done, introducing mundane and nefarious considerations into a mood that she might have regarded as holy. Whatever it was, she evidently changed her mind. She spoke with controlled passion.

"I said I would deal with it."

"I know. But he has business experience, and so have I. I thought I might help."

"You should concentrate on your own side."

I wish I had done more thinking.

I thought how far we had travelled since the time when I had got part-time work with Mr Wether and she had opposed me because I would not tell the Social Security about it.

"I will."

She walked forward across the room, to the small table we had brought and on which she had put her tape and her measurements for curtains and carpets. "I think it is time we went home now."

I made nothing of this incident.

There were others. If I listed them all, it would seem impossible that I did not make more of them or inquire about their meaning. But that would only be the illusion which is engendered by any telling. To see them in perspective, and to see how small they were in relation to all the rest of our life, I would have to give all the happenings of all the days in full, and recount the detail of several weeks, all of which would be pointless.

I was happy in the way I was that day when I went back

to have lunch at the Bull. I was also buying a new car, with all the modesty and determination not to spend unnecessary money. I could spend weeks, literally, reading magazine reports and comparing design features, and even idly jotting down figures that would enable me to compare the thermal efficiency of an engine. I did not have to be told that these things did not matter greatly. On the other hand, the very opposite of what I wanted to do was to splash out a lot of money, and then have trouble and be left with a feeling for years that I had not done the right thing. It is a characteristic of active happiness to be blind, and most men, given the time, a new house, a new car to think of, to say nothing of a young mistress who had just discovered bed, would be fully occupied, very content with the way things were going, and no different in their worldly preoccupations from the very ordinary way that I was.

27

I WOULD LIKE to slide into it, really.

It was on the day that I walked to Delicia's that it happened. There was no question of us going to bed that night. At least, I had learned when I had gone there a couple of nights before, there was no question of her having a child, which was luck, for we had been incautious the first time. I had a message to give her. In a fortnight, the remover's van would arrive, and we would be going to Penfolds. I would be seeing her all the time then. I looked out at the evening, intending to go with the car, when the kind of night that it was changed my mind. "I think I'll walk," I told Margaret.

It says something about my state of mind that after using the car for a month, I was starting to realize that a change had occurred, and that I was missing something from the time I used to walk or cycle everywhere. I could afford to wonder about my health and whether I would get fat.

There was nothing of importance except the final news to give to Delicia, and she only wished to tell me how her father was coming home drunk almost every night, and she was worried by the change in his habits. So was I. At the rate he was going, he would soon get through the money I had given him and start asking for more. But I could not discuss it with her. It was a point on which I could no more be frank than anyone normally could, when people talked of their relatives. Had I been, I would have had to tell her that I hoped he would drink himself to death, and the sooner the better. She was a little bored, and consequently boring. I made the fact that I had come on foot and had to walk back across the town an excuse to leave early.

In fact I found it interesting to walk across Lockley, out by one route and back by another. We were approaching the lightest nights of the year, and even when I was coming back there were groups of young people, the boys sometimes talking or laughing loudly and the girls egging them on, parading or standing about between the closed shops in the sunset. I walked through them and noticed how, intent as they were on one another, they did not see any person over fifty. I thought it was the kind of scene that could probably have taken place in Lockley a hundred years ago, or a thousand. As I believed had happened in Athens a lot earlier, only the most forward girls were there risking their reputations, listening to the outrageous and blasphemous things the boys said. I was sceptical about how different modern life was.

I suppose I am saying that I felt I was in a position to see life clearly and to see it whole, which is what any successful man feels. I was now successful. How I now hate it.

The sun had set, but it was still full daylight with a pleasant glow to the north-west as I came up the hill to the Drive. I had a feeling of virtue, for when I got home I would have walked four miles. The traffic was spasmodic on the main road, and during the intervals I could hear plenty of birdsong and a late lawn-mower going somewhere. It seemed a long way up the hill but I eventually came to Derrington Drive with the telephone and the pillar box on the corner. I was just wondering if it would be the last time I would see them from this vantage point, since it was not very likely that I would walk up there again and in a car it was necessary to keep one's eyes on the traffic, when I became aware that there was a white ambulance in the Drive. It was stationary.

I do not know why I quickened my pace a little. We had plenty of old people in Derrington Drive. Nor, when they were taken to or from their homes by ambulance, were they always severe cases. It just looked as though it were stopped in my section, somewhere near my house.

Impossible thoughts crossed my mind as they do at such times. I thought that Margaret might have committed suicide. This was obviously quite crazy. Then I thought she might have had an accident. In fact this seemed ridiculous. There was no reason she should, in the house. She was much less likely to have been taken ill than the other people in the vicinity. The thoughts were inspired, or at least not contradicted, by the fact that as I walked down the road it became clearer that the ambulance was stopped either at my house or McFarlane's.

McFarlane's, I thought. That would not be a surprise. In any event, there was no saying that the ambulance would actually stop at the house for which it was intended. Having second thoughts, I could see no reason why I should think those things about Margaret. It was a little disturbing that I should have done so. I could see no reason for them.

A man, one of the ambulance men, came out of a house and garden and went to the ambulance. He did something in the driver's seat, and then at the back. I was nearer by this time. I was also walking faster though I was telling myself that there was no need for me to do so. It had looked, most uncomfortably for a moment, as though that man had come out of my house.

I think it was at that point that I almost broke into a run. It had become clear gradually that the ambulance was definitely at my gate, and as I cleared the Belfonts' tall hedge, I could see that it was my front door that was wide open. I had a new kind of fatal feeling that could only be described as not-thinking.

The ambulance man came towards me. Coming from the ambulance he appeared to think he had some right to stop me. He put out a hand and said, "Don't go in there, sir!" I went straight past him, and right in.

From the hall, I heard low voices. At least two people were

talking, and in a hushed way. The living-room door was open, and I only stopped on the threshold to take in and feel relief at the scene before me, with McFarlane stretched out there.

Margaret was standing, and all right. Mary McFarlane was in a chair. The Misses Cleveland were present, another ambulance man, and the doctor. I got it. I felt relief. It looked like a death scene. But only McFarlane.

Mary McFarlane was sobbing, controlled in collapse, and the Misses Cleveland were standing with her attentively, around what was normally my chair. McFarlane was apparently not dead. The doctor and the ambulance man were working at him on a stretcher, on which he had apparently been picked up and then put down again just before he got to the door. To me, it looked as though they were giving him artificial respiration and an injection at the same time. And Margaret was stood by the sideboard. I did not feel it was quite right.

I went into the room. For some reason, I felt I must get to Margaret. It had something to do with her look, or that reinforced it. I do not think it was only that I had to convince myself that she was not the one on the stretcher.

I kept close to the wall. I was very careful not to touch anyone. As it was, without looking at me, the doctor said, "Can't you keep clear?" He was also our doctor. I realized that he was doing what he could, but there was defeat in his voice, like someone trying to re-start a stopped heart. I thought that Mary McFarlane would get bad news in a minute. Once clear, I was able to look at Margaret. She stood by two glasses of wine on the sideboard.

I was in the state in which one notices peculiarly small things. I noticed the bottle by the glasses. It was an apéritif that Stephanie and David had brought with them for Christmas, and that we still had because no one liked it. It had an exceptionally vile taste. I had almost reached Margaret.

Mary McFarlane stopped watching her husband. It seemed

likely that she had come to the same conclusion as I had. She looked across the room in our direction, and pointed at Margaret.

"You did it!" she said in a high voice. "You've killed him!"

I had not noticed that Mary McFarlane was jealous of Margaret with McFarlane before. I saw it now, but I could not see how Margaret could be accused of killing him. I did not understand it. I noticed Margaret just stood there.

"Mary, you must not say such things," Daisy Cleveland said, and put her hand on the older woman's shoulder as though to push down the arm that still pointed.

I felt a familiar feeling of sickness.

"She gave him a drink," Mary McFarlane said. "She gave him a drink without asking me. At his age and in his condition." Her voice dropped, and she said more to the Misses Cleveland, but it was unintelligible. I tried hard to hear it.

I looked at Margaret, to see how she responded to being accused. To me it sounded unlikely. I could see no reason for her giving McFarlane a drink. At the same time, there were the glasses and the bottle on the sideboard. She was standing stiff and upright a little away from the sideboard and looking at the doctor and McFarlane. She must have heard McFarlane's wife, but she took no apparent notice, so I looked where she did. I felt I knew something.

Dr Hewitt, who was kneeling by his patient, looked up I could see he was going to lose his battle, and he looked around for someone to blame. He saw me and recognized me. He said, "Can you get people out? This room is crowded."

I looked at the group at the chair, and saw that unless it were possible to get Mary McFarlane out first, which looked unlikely, I was not going to shift them. That left myself and Margaret and the ambulance man. I touched Margaret on the arm, and then took it and propelled her. We went out to the kitchen.

I pushed the door closed. We were alone. For the first time, I asked her, "What happened?" I dare not speak loudly.

Margaret looked at me. "I found the apéritif while I was clearing the house. I thought we didn't want to take it to Penfolds. I saw McFarlane in his garden. I called him over and asked him if he wanted the bottle. He said he didn't know, so I said, 'Then come in and taste it.' It turned out that Mary would not let him have it. He drank one, and then asked for another. He collapsed. I am at fault, Dalby."

The story seemed clear and genuine enough. I looked again at Margaret. I looked more carefully.

"The people in there?"

"I ran out. I could do nothing with him. The Misses Cleveland were passing."

Margaret was calm and collected. There was just the way she looked, and a note. She could be reciting.

I felt fear. Our eyes met. Hers did not look away but they did not answer the question that mine asked. I felt fear before I knew any reason. I thought suddenly: Margaret.

She moved and made a gesture and glanced at the door. I put out a hand to stop her. She said, "Dalby, I must go back in there."

"Why?" There were a million things I wanted to know though she had apparently given me all the answers.

She spoke with so much conviction that I could no longer stop her. "I must go back in there!" She went, and I was looking at the door. I felt shocked and unthinking.

I thought: Margaret. Margaret with her high principles and dignity and pride. Margaret who would rather have starved than let me lie to the Social Security people. But there was also the Margaret on whom I had imposed what was to her the most abject humiliation. I looked at the door. I was not going to stay out if no one else did. I went back into the room.

Something had happened. It was like a jerk in a film, where events had made progress. The doctor was not where he had been. He was standing over Mary McFarlane. The Misses Cleveland were attentive. It was the ambulance man who was dealing, without haste, with the body that was stretched out flat on the floor. Margaret was standing, where she had been. The doctor was saying, "You knew it was bound to happen one day, Mrs McFarlane."

Without lifting her head, Mary McFarlane said, "She—" Margaret watched her.

The doctor said, "Now come, Mrs McFarlane." He looked up at us. He was no longer in haste and he did not order people out. "We'd better get her home," he said. He considered a situation he regarded as doubtful. "Unless she can stay here?"

Daisy Cleveland touched his arm and looked with sympathy and understanding at Margaret. "We will take her home." She explained to the doctor. "It will be better for the moment."

The doctor stood up and looked around. It seemed to him that he should apologize to Margaret. "She is distraught, I am afraid. Perhaps if Miss Cleveland . . ."

I was telling myself, it is all right. It is all right. I watched old Dr Hewitt talk to the ambulance man, whose mate, who had tried to stop me coming in, was at the door of the room. He was apparently correcting them about the destination of the body. "No, next door. I'll show you." They all moved. They organized themselves, and it took a little time. I had seen death before, my father's. (It was impossible to count deaths in wartime, that took place out of sight of the women who wept.)

It seemed a moment, and then Margaret and I stood in the room watching the doctor, the ambulance men with the stretcher, the Misses Cleveland and Mary McFarlane, virtually a cortège, go down the path past the window. The room seemed suddenly empty yet under pressure, like a diving bell, a chamber.

Margaret moved then, when she saw them securely past the

gate. She made no attempt to conceal what she was doing. Perhaps she knew it was too late. She turned to the sideboard with a quick motion and looked narrowly at the glasses. Without a look at me, she picked one of them up delicately, paused only an instant, and then went off to the kitchen, holding the glass between thumb and forefinger. I watched her actions as though I had expected them, though I had not been sure until then. I heard the gurgle of liquid poured out in the sink, then the kitchen tap start to run. I looked at the kitchen door. I went towards the other glass on the sideboard and looked at it, then before she came back I felt I knew. I opened the door of the cupboard where the glasses were kept.

It was as though I knew what I would find there. It was out of sight round the side of the cupboard, but I put my hand to it. It was the bottle of Cousin Mavis's medicine. Mavis had a heart condition too, but she neither looked nor behaved like McFarlane. I thought: Digitalis.

The apéritif bottle stood on the sideboard, a dark liquid with a strong sweet-and-sour taste that, especially to anyone who was not familiar with it, would disguise any flavour. I was looking at it with the medicine bottle in my hand when Margaret came back. She went past me to the sideboard and put the glass back. From the bottle that was there, she partly refilled it. I thought, with her rigidity of outlook, I had seen it before. When rigid people were pressed, they did not bend like the rest. They broke, it was like a fracture, and there was nothing to stop them. I had never imagined.

The replaced and refilled glass was innocent. She had dried it after she had washed it, and it stood on the sideboard looking just as it had been. It was there for when the doctor came back.

"Why did you do it?" I said.

She turned and looked at me rigidly. She looked entirely herself, her face firm with all the lines I remembered. She spoke as clearly as she said anything else.

"I had to. He found out."

She did not know, probably no one would know, that to have killed McFarlane, an old man who would soon die, was something I would not have done myself. It was a thousand times, it was incomparably worse, to have brought Margaret to the point where she did it. I saw all the past.

It seemed very still in the room with only the two of us there, standing quite close together. I thought: I had broken the rules. Like a child learning his first innocent lesson, I had not seen that others would also do the same thing. It had been I alone who was clever.

"You should have left it to me."

"It was you who made a mess of it, Dalby. The story you told him." Her look summed me up.

I had a picture, a mental vision, of McFarlane standing in his garden, with his *Daily Telegraph* under his arm. McFarlane the earnest, self-opinionated, interfering citizen. I had told him what? That Margaret's money was a bequest, that it was not in the will. What was it, some small thing?

"He thought we were liable for death duties," Margaret said, looking at me. "I would have to have got the money over seven years ago if we were not."

I looked around. I made a gesture towards next door. I said, "Mary McFarlane...?"

Margaret's face expressed scorn. "You don't think this is the first time I've had him in here? I had to find out his intentions. He believed there was a tax-fraud in the Kingsman estate. He was going to write to the papers."

I felt a searing descent. It was not only that I had forced it on her, and brought her to do it. I had caused her and forced her and not in any way helped her.

Margaret took the medicine bottle from my hand and began to walk away with it to the kitchen. It was the moment of my life. Thinking what? That those who broke the rules were responsible for the results of all of their actions? It was not thinking. It was the sight of her familiar back as she walked. It was the look of her grey hair.

It had nothing to do with the anguish of fated desires and ideals that you cannot undo things.

28

As THOUGH LIFE were the same. As though the dead were still speaking.

I suppose the only thing remaining to tell is how we live now at Penfolds. Oh, yes, we live here, there has been nothing to stop us, in this house with its open sheltered landscape and its view of the headland and sea. The dream has put on flesh, except that it is a question of whether it is a dream or a nightmare.

I sit here at this window in August, and I have just started writing. It is the right way, as I understand it from the little I know, to write the last chapter first. But I do not write for pleasure or literary ambition. I write for a purpose.

I can see a too-pleasant scene from this window. I look at the people sunbathing on the beach, and my thoughts try to wander. Looking at the people and the cove, I wonder in what impossible places they have left their cars, and whether it is in my drive. I look again at the sea and the rocks where they sit, and I think that their near-naked bodies look natural there, as they do nowhere else. I sit shivering, slightly.

They *are* natural, just as we are "natural" after taking steps with our lives that are in advance of our times, and that I believe are being taken by other people more slowly. They do not look as though they have high principles as they lie in the cove. I imagine they have. They would be horrified if they knew who and what lives in this house they can see on the hillside. But it would do them no good, and it would serve them no purpose; it would only cost them money in taxes, and it would be a charade to denounce us.

It is not that I have not seen and understood, nor that I failed to think. We must go back to the rules. I could not imagine it, that was all, to have Margaret arrested, not even when we stood in the rain, as we did, among the mourners, by the open grave of McFarlane. I would not have gone. I saw what it would be like, with Mary McFarlane looking through us and somehow proclaiming in her grief that she blamed Margaret for what she saw as seduction and debauchery and death of her near-eighty-year-old-husband. It was Margaret who made us.

Looking at her by the grave, I thought, if she knew! I saw Margaret in the dock, in a court, in a cell, and always flanked or surrounded by warders. I thought, No, and I found it incredible. What good would it do? At the funeral I knew we could not go that way.

We cannot go back, and looking at the cliffs and the specks of people on the headland, I think this is the trouble. The world, and not only us, cannot go back from the way that we think now. It has something to do with the way that we live. The idea of punishment and vengeance is too primitive, too related to the past, to some old-time shepherds perhaps, who came here with bows and arrows and stalked one another, in their feuds, in this landscape. We live in a different world, in which people come down to the sea and these rocks in their cars, and they choose this cove because their children can run naked, and young housewives who have been abroad can lie in costumes that are topless, and there are no policemen. At midnight, a car will arrive and we hear the voices of young men, and look out at the laughter of young girls as they run down to the sea and bathe in the moonlight with bodies like shadows on silver. There is silence, they have disappeared among the rocks, but the car still remains there. Even for the other young ones, the wreckers, who had twice broken our gate, vengeance has become aimless, and too lost and transient an emotion.

I believe I thought, Oh, no! and Not now! when a policeman knocked us up only five days after the funeral, and stood on our doorstep. I was being asked for, he announced to my panic. There had been an accident, and a man called Dobson had been killed, and it was his daughter who was asking. The policeman, whom I asked in while I dressed, did not say that Dobson was drunk. He had come staggering out of a pub—perhaps I knew it was ill-lighted that street?—and been knocked down by a car. Yes, the driver had been given a breath-test, and there would probably be charges. While I put on my coat, I said, Yes, I knew the Dobsons, I knew that the daughter was a cripple, she could not manage the stairs, and would be alone in the house. I was thinking: Charge the driver? It was I who had killed Dobson—Dobson too!—by the money I gave him. The policeman was the crudity of the law; while, for people who knew no laws, there was no alternative but that a man should be responsible for the results of all of his actions.

I had thought, and been thinking all the time until then, that I could not bring Delicia to Penfolds. She is down there in the garden now. In this summer-still house, where the windows are open to the bees, I can hear the clink of Margaret preparing food in the kitchen below. Delicia, down the slope of the garden, works along a path in her wheel-chair in sunlight, and with a garden tool cuts off the dead heads of the roses. At the time of McFarlane's funeral, standing in the rain, I had thought: Margaret is a murderess. I am married to a murderess. All the words had old meanings. Now I cannot, now it would be insane to bring my young mistress to live in the same house. I had been putting off seeing her when the call of Dobson's death came, dreading it, and not knowing how I could tell her. It was impossible. I could see it.

I should have known better than to think that, in today's world when reality is changing and one scene dissolves and slides into another, there is any such thing as "impossible" or "cannot".

At daybreak at the Dobsons' I arranged for a woman from

the street to come in, to stay with Delicia. I still did not know what I was going to do. I went to the social services, to the offices of the council. Delicia had no one else, unless her mother could be contacted. No, she could not manage the stairs. I went from one office to another, speaking to people who would accept no responsibility, who were officials who regarded their work as to do with printed regulations, not people, which is another thing these days. It was a harassed elderly woman whom I came to in the end. She looked at my suit and listened to the names of important people in the town that I was dropping. She was willing but unable. "It is a question of vacancies." All the people I had mentioned, who might take an interest, were those who opposed any increase in the rates. "Where do you expect us to put her?" The only institutions there were, were for the deformed and the mongols and the sub-normal children. Or should she go to the other places, for the mentally-deficient adults, or the aged and the senile? When I said something about the inadequate provision of Lockley, she turned on me furiously. "Do you think this is only in Lockley? Until you see a case at first hand, you think of nothing but roads and police, and the provision of university places for your children who could live well enough if they had no education whatever." I came away. She called after me. "Why don't you take the girl in your own home? You will get an allowance."

It had an effect on me that she, a total stranger, should see it in that way. The risk? It was up to me to take the risk, and not tell Delicia what she risked. If I had any ability it was to deal with a situation from one day to the next. There need not be friction, if I watched it from moment to moment, for the rest of my lifetime.

It has come to me recently that if we had taken on Delicia, and one or two others, during our bad days at Derrington Drive, we could possibly have lived there on what came in from our incomes, though to the outrage of neighbours. I look outwards.

We live peacefully here, at least so far. Margaret, "the murderess," has not undergone that change that seems to be accepted with the title in fiction. She still looks the same, she behaves in the same way she always has, and is still the same person. It is possible that for two thousand or three thousand years, since the nomad Jewish tribes invented their outraged God, the Almighty God of Wrath, that the whole world has been living a fiction? I do not know. It is frighteningly easy to invent realities, but infinitely difficult and tortuous, and frightening, to live from day to day and find out. This afternoon Margaret will go shopping in the car. I have to balance the risk that if I let her go alone she is a very bad driver. It is not likely that I will stay here alone with Delicia, since Margaret takes it for granted that I will go with her and drive her. If there is a suggestion over lunch that maybe I should go with a list to the grocers, I must have some reason ready why we cannot do it that way. There is no question of me going out to work, even if employment were offered. It may or may not be, it is my guilty conscience that tells me that it would be unwise to leave them alone. Every day I have to arrange things afresh, and today it may end with me putting Delicia in the car, and taking her, or Margaret, or both of them together, for our twice-weekly shopping in Lockley, safe for a short time.

We have only had the summer here so far, and only the best of it at that. I do not know what it will be like in this lonely place when for days on end the rain shrouds the landscape, the winter gales blow in from the sea, the cove is empty of people, and we are virtually cut off. Then indeed the dream may gradually turn into a nightmare. But I will be here, and have taken the responsibility on myself, and must find out, by waiting.

At the moment, while the summer lasts, I am writing this narrative for reasons, and yet with foreboding. One is not strong. I have seen, in a local paper, that the police have new evidence in the case of the burglary at Lawson's. Someone heard a car start, and it has been established that it was before the explosion, not after. I do not think that anything will come of this. I do not see how it can now. The law is at once too blunt, and has been made too tortuous by lawyers. The amount of evidence and false clues that I left in even my simpler crimes would provide a field-day for the wealthy, opposing articulate counsels, if it ever came to a trial. Even certainty on the part of the police would not be enough, for the confusion of the jury would be such that they could not get a conviction.

Mary McFarlane is different. She still lives in Derrington Drive, and even at some risk, I sometimes go there to hear of her widow's talk from the Clevelands and Belfonts. She is a woman without intelligence or reason, and her story is still not coherent. She is convinced that Margaret Pearson, when her own husband was discovered to have interests elsewhere, made a bid for her husband. When she found she could not get him, though she enticed him into her house, she did "something". The story has been growing as Mary McFarlane tells it, and she has once mentioned "poison".

This is not dangerous as it stands, but it could be, if anyone could be persuaded by repetition to check up on us, and were to discover that Margaret did not get money from her uncle. It is possible that one solid fact of that kind could somehow undo us, though I can hardly believe it.

I look down at Delicia in the garden. She has completed her row of roses, and has pushed her garden shears in the bars of her chair. She is moving off along the zig-zag slopes that I have provided with paths, and is going to talk to some young people who have stopped at our gate. It has come to me recently that I do not know Delicia. I have been infatuated with her, which is almost the same as not knowing.

Why have I not told her of her danger? From that at least I have held back, and as I look at her, I am not sure why. Is it because the one time I saw Delicia clearly was when I first met her, and at that time the one clear thing I saw was that she was not above blackmail?

Blackmail, Delicia? We have a murderess and a thief in the same house. Everything is peaceful, and yet sometimes I think that my realities are shifting.

The money I have will barely last Margaret's and my lifetimes. There is always the chance that, in case of my arrest, it might be seized and returned. This is a reality I understand, and I cannot let matters rest as they are without taking out insurance. The insurance is this writing.

The law, I believe, if I were arrested, would take back the money, and all we have, to make restitution. But not money made after the arrest. I wonder what this manuscript will be worth to the Sunday papers, "written up" by ghost writers?

There is also the thought that I may die prematurely. It would be foolish not to think of it, while living in a house with Margaret's high principles, and a young, prattling mistress.

This is the year 1974 in which I write. This narrative will go to the bank and be kept in a safe place. I believe I have everything under control, and no disasters will happen. I think I have learned wisdom, and that my outlook on life is a real one. I certainly hope so. If Margaret were to learn why Delicia is here and that there is no Mr Wether at all, it could be on Delicia and me both that she would exact vengeance.

If all goes well, this never need see daylight at all, or at least it should not be published until my natural death, perhaps in the late 1990s.

If it is published before then? I do not know. There is always the urge to make money. And maybe to point out how the world is from one view. For that alone, if anyone would listen, it might be worth while to change our names, and change all the place-names.

Penfolds,
Penfold,
1974

THE PERENNIAL LIBRARY MYSTERY SERIES

Delano Ames

CORPSE DIPLOMATIQUE   P 637, $2.84
"Sprightly and intelligent."

—*New York Herald Tribune Book Review*

FOR OLD CRIME'S SAKE   P 629, $2.84

MURDER, MAESTRO, PLEASE   P 630, $2.84
"If there is a more engaging couple in modern fiction than Jane and Dagobert Brown, we have not met them."   —*Scotsman*

SHE SHALL HAVE MURDER   P 638, $2.84
"Combines the merit of both the English and American schools in the new mystery. It's as breezy as the best of the American ones, and has the sophistication and wit of any top-notch Britisher."

—*New York Herald Tribune Book Review*

E. C. Bentley

TRENT'S LAST CASE   P 440, $2.50
"One of the three best detective stories ever written."

—*Agatha Christie*

TRENT'S OWN CASE   P 516, $2.25
"I won't waste time saying that the plot is sound and the detection satisfying. Trent has not altered a scrap and reappears with all his old humor and charm."

—*Dorothy L. Sayers*

Gavin Black

A DRAGON FOR CHRISTMAS   P 473, $1.95
"Potent excitement!"

—*New York Herald Tribune*

THE EYES AROUND ME   P 485, $1.95
"I stayed up until all hours last night reading *The Eyes Around Me,* which is something I do not do very often, but I was so intrigued by the ingeniousness of Mr. Black's plotting and the witty way in which he spins his mystery. I can only say that I enjoyed the book enormously."

—*F. van Wyck Mason*

YOU WANT TO DIE, JOHNNY?   P 472, $1.95
"Gavin Black doesn't just develop a pressure plot in suspense, he adds uninfected wit, character, charm, and sharp knowledge of the Far East to make rereading as keen as the first race-through."   —*Book Week*

Nicholas Blake

THE CORPSE IN THE SNOWMAN   P 427, $1.95
"If there is a distinction between the novel and the detective story (which
we do not admit), then this book deserves a high place in both catego-
ries."   —*The New York Times*

THE DREADFUL HOLLOW   P 493, $1.95
"Pace unhurried, characters excellent, reasoning solid."
                                                —*San Francisco Chronicle*

END OF CHAPTER   P 397, $1.95
". . . admirably solid . . . an adroit formal detective puzzle backed up
by firm characterization and a knowing picture of London publishing."
                                                —*The New York Times*

HEAD OF A TRAVELER   P 398, $2.25
"Another grade A detective story of the right old jigsaw persuasion."
                                                —*New York Herald Tribune Book Review*

MINUTE FOR MURDER   P 419, $1.95
"An outstanding mystery novel. Mr. Blake's writing is a delight in
itself."
                                                —*The New York Times*

THE MORNING AFTER DEATH   P 520, $1.95
"One of Blake's best."
                                                —Rex Warner

A PENKNIFE IN MY HEART   P 521, $2.25
"Style brilliant . . . and suspenseful."   —*San Francisco Chronicle*

THE PRIVATE WOUND   P 531, $2.25
[Blake's] best novel in a dozen years . . . . An intensely penetrating study
of sexual passion. . . . A powerful story of murder and its aftermath."
                                                —Anthony Boucher, *The New York Times*

A QUESTION OF PROOF   P 494, $1.95
"The characters in this story are unusually well drawn, and the suspense
is well sustained."   —*The New York Times*

THE SAD VARIETY   P 495, $2.25
"It is a stunner. I read it instead of eating, instead of sleeping."
                                                —Dorothy Salisbury Davis

THERE'S TROUBLE BREWING   P 569, $3.37
"Nigel Strangeways is a puzzling mixture of simplicity and penetration,
but all the more real for that."   —*The Times Literary Supplement*

THOU SHELL OF DEATH   P 428, $1.95

"It has all the virtues of culture, intelligence and sensibility that the most exacting connoisseur could ask of detective fiction."

—*The Times* [London] *Literary Supplement*

THE WIDOW'S CRUISE   P 399, $2.25

"A stirring suspense. . . . The thrilling tale leaves nothing to be desired."

—*Springfield Republican*

THE WORM OF DEATH   P 400, $2.25

"It [The Worm of Death] is one of Blake's very best—and his best is better than almost anyone's."   —Louis Untermeyer

John & Emery Bonett

A BANNER FOR PEGASUS   P 554, $2.40

"A gem! Beautifully plotted and set. . . . Not only is the murder adroit and deserved, and the detection competent, but the love story is charming."   —Jacques Barzun and Wendell Hertig Taylor

DEAD LION   P 563, $2.40

"A clever plot, authentic background and interesting characters highly recommended this one."   —*New Republic*

Christianna Brand

GREEN FOR DANGER   P 551, $2.50

"You have to reach for the greatest of Great Names (Christie, Carr, Queen . . .) to find Brand's rivals in the devious subtleties of the trade."

—Anthony Boucher

TOUR DE FORCE   P 572, $2.40

"Complete with traps for the over-ingenious, a double-reverse surprise ending and a key clue planted so fairly and obviously that you completely overlook it. If that's your idea of perfect entertainment, then seize at once upon *Tour de Force.*"   —Anthony Boucher, *The New York Times*

James Byrom

OR BE HE DEAD   P 585, $2.84

"A very original tale . . . Well written and steadily entertaining."

—Jacques Barzun & Wendell Hertig Taylor, *A Catalogue of Crime*

Henry Calvin

IT'S DIFFERENT ABROAD   P 640, $2.84
"What is remarkable and delightful, Mr. Calvin imparts a flavor of satire
to what he renovates and compels us to take straight."

—Jacques Barzun

Marjorie Carleton

VANISHED   P 559, $2.40
"Exceptional . . . a minor triumph."
—Jacques Barzun and Wendell Hertig Taylor, *A Catalogue of Crime*

George Harmon Coxe

MURDER WITH PICTURES   P 527, $2.25
"[Coxe] has hit the bull's-eye with his first shot."

—*The New York Times*

Edmund Crispin

BURIED FOR PLEASURE   P 506, $2.50
"Absolute and unalloyed delight."

—Anthony Boucher, *The New York Times*

Lionel Davidson

THE MENORAH MEN   P 592, $2.84
"Of his fellow thriller writers, only John Le Carré shows the same
instinct for the viscera."   —*Chicago Tribune*

NIGHT OF WENCESLAS   P 595, $2.84
"A most ingenious thriller, so enriched with style, wit, and a sense of
serious comedy that it all but transcends its kind."

—*The New Yorker*

THE ROSE OF TIBET   P 593, $2.84
"I hadn't realized how much I missed the genuine Adventure story
. . . until I read *The Rose of Tibet*."   —Graham Greene

D. M. Devine

MY BROTHER'S KILLER   P 558, $2.40
"A most enjoyable crime story which I enjoyed reading down to the last
moment."   —Agatha Christie

Kenneth Fearing

THE BIG CLOCK P 500, $1.95

"It will be some time before chill-hungry clients meet again so rare a compound of irony, satire, and icy-fingered narrative. *The Big Clock* is . . . a psychothriller you won't put down." —*Weekly Book Review*

Andrew Garve

THE ASHES OF LODA P 430, $1.50

"Garve . . . embellishes a fine fast adventure story with a more credible picture of the U.S.S.R. than is offered in most thrillers."
—*The New York Times Book Review*

THE CUCKOO LINE AFFAIR P 451, $1.95

". . . an agreeable and ingenious piece of work." —*The New Yorker*

A HERO FOR LEANDA P 429, $1.50

"One can trust Mr. Garve to put a fresh twist to any situation, and the ending is really a lovely surprise." —*The Manchester Guardian*

MURDER THROUGH THE LOOKING GLASS P 449, $1.95

". . . refreshingly out-of-the-way and enjoyable . . . highly recommended to all comers." —*Saturday Review*

NO TEARS FOR HILDA P 441, $1.95

"It starts fine and finishes finer. I got behind on breathing watching Max get not only his man but his woman, too." —Rex Stout

THE RIDDLE OF SAMSON P 450, $1.95

"The story is an excellent one, the people are quite likable, and the writing is superior." —*Springfield Republican*

Michael Gilbert

BLOOD AND JUDGMENT P 446, $1.95

"Gilbert readers need scarcely be told that the characters all come alive at first sight, and that his surpassing talent for narration enhances any plot. . . . Don't miss." —*San Francisco Chronicle*

THE BODY OF A GIRL P 459, $1.95

"Does what a good mystery should do: open up into all kinds of ramifications, with untold menace behind the action. At the end, there is a bang-up climax, and it is a pleasure to see how skilfully Gilbert wraps everything up." —*The New York Times Book Review*

THE DANGER WITHIN P 448, $1.95
"Michael Gilbert has nicely combined some elements of the straight detective story with plenty of action, suspense, and adventure, to produce a superior thriller." —*Saturday Review*

FEAR TO TREAD P 458, $1.95
"Merits serious consideration as a work of art."

—*The New York Times*

Joe Gores

HAMMETT P 631, $2.84
"Joe Gores at his very best. Terse, powerful writing—with the master, Dashiell Hammett, as the protagonist in a novel I think he would have been proud to call his own." —*Robert Ludlum*

C. W. Grafton

BEYOND A REASONABLE DOUBT P 519, $1.95
"A very ingenious tale of murder . . . a brilliant and gripping narrative."
—*Jacques Barzun and Wendell Hertig Taylor*

THE RAT BEGAN TO GNAW THE ROPE P 639, $2.84
"Fast, humorous story with flashes of brilliance."

—*The New Yorker*

Edward Grierson

THE SECOND MAN P 528, $2.25
"One of the best trial-testimony books to have come along in quite a while." —*The New Yorker*

Bruce Hamilton

TOO MUCH OF WATER P 635, $2.84
"A superb sea mystery. . . . The prose is excellent."
—*Jacques Barzun and Wendell Hertig Taylor, A Catalogue of Crime*

Cyril Hare

DEATH IS NO SPORTSMAN P 555, $2.40
"You will be thrilled because it succeeds in placing an ingenious story in a new and refreshing setting. . . . The identity of the murderer is really a surprise." —*Daily Mirror*

DEATH WALKS THE WOODS P 556, $2.40
"Here is a fine formal detective story, with a technically brilliant solution demanding the attention of all connoisseurs of construction."
—Anthony Boucher, *The New York Times Book Review*

AN ENGLISH MURDER P 455, $2.50
"By a long shot, the best crime story I have read for a long time. Everything is traditional, but originality does not suffer. The setting is perfect. Full marks to Mr. Hare." —*Irish Press*

SUICIDE EXCEPTED P 636, $2.84
"Adroit in its manipulation . . . and distinguished by a plot-twister which I'll wager Christie wishes she'd thought of."
—*The New York Times*

TENANT FOR DEATH P 570, $2.84
"The way in which an air of probability is combined both with clear, terse narrative and with a good deal of subtle suburban atmosphere, proves the extreme skill of the writer." —*The Spectator*

TRAGEDY AT LAW P 522, $2.25
"An extremely urbane and well-written detective story."
—*The New York Times*

UNTIMELY DEATH P 514, $2.25
"The English detective story at its quiet best, meticulously underplayed, rich in perceivings of the droll human animal and ready at the last with a neat surprise which has been there all the while had we but wits to see it." —*New York Herald Tribune Book Review*

THE WIND BLOWS DEATH P 589, $2.84
"A plot compounded of musical knowledge, a Dickens allusion, and a subtle point in law is related with delightfully unobtrusive wit, warmth, and style." —*The New York Times*

WITH A BARE BODKIN P 523, $2.25
"One of the best detective stories published for a long time."
—*The Spectator*

Robert Harling

THE ENORMOUS SHADOW P 545, $2.50
"In some ways the best spy story of the modern period. . . . The writing is terse and vivid . . . the ending full of action . . . altogether first-rate."
—Jacques Barzun and Wendell Hertig Taylor, *A Catalogue of Crime*

Matthew Head

THE CABINDA AFFAIR   P 541, $2.25
"An absorbing whodunit and a distinguished novel of atmosphere."
— Anthony Boucher, *The New York Times*

THE CONGO VENUS   P 597, $2.84
"Terrific. The dialogue is just plain wonderful."
— *The Boston Globe*

MURDER AT THE FLEA CLUB   P 542, $2.50
"The true delight is in Head's style, its limpid ease combined with humor
and an awesome precision of phrase."   — *San Francisco Chronicle*

M. V. Heberden

ENGAGED TO MURDER   P 533, $2.25
"Smooth plotting."   — *The New York Times*

James Hilton

WAS IT MURDER?   P 501, $1.95
"The story is well planned and well written."
— *The New York Times*

P. M. Hubbard

HIGH TIDE   P 571, $2.40
"A smooth elaboration of mounting horror and danger."
— *Library Journal*

Elspeth Huxley

THE AFRICAN POISON MURDERS   P 540, $2.25
"Obscure venom, manical mutilations, deadly bush fire, thrilling climax
compose major opus.... Top-flight."
— *Saturday Review of Literature*

MURDER ON SAFARI   P 587, $2.84
"Right now we'd call Mrs. Huxley a dangerous rival to Agatha Christie."   — *Books*

Francis Iles

BEFORE THE FACT P 517, $2.50

"Not many 'serious' novelists have produced character studies to compare with Iles's internally terrifying portrait of the murderer in *Before the Fact,* his masterpiece and a work truly deserving the appellation of unique and beyond price."
—Howard Haycraft

MALICE AFORETHOUGHT P 532, $1.95

"It is a long time since I have read anything so good as *Malice Aforethought,* with its cynical humour, acute criminology, plausible detail and rapid movement. It makes you hug yourself with pleasure."
—H. C. Harwood, *Saturday Review*

Michael Innes

THE CASE OF THE JOURNEYING BOY P 632, $3.12

"I could see no faults in it. There is no one to compare with him."
—*Illustrated London News*

DEATH BY WATER P 574, $2.40

"The amount of ironic social criticism and deft characterization of scenes and people would serve another author for six books."
—Jacques Barzun and Wendell Hertig Taylor

HARE SITTING UP P 590, $2.84

"There is hardly anyone (in mysteries or mainstream) more exquisitely literate, allusive and Jamesian—and hardly anyone with a firmer sense of melodramatic plot or a more vigorous gift of storytelling."
—Anthony Boucher, *The New York Times*

THE LONG FAREWELL P 575, $2.40

"A model of the deft, classic detective story, told in the most wittily diverting prose."
—*The New York Times*

THE MAN FROM THE SEA P 591, $2.84

"The pace is brisk, the adventures exciting and excitingly told, and above all he keeps to the very end the interesting ambiguity of the man from the sea."
—*New Statesman*

THE SECRET VANGUARD P 584, $2.84

"Innes . . . has mastered the art of swift, exciting and well-organized narrative."
—*The New York Times*

THE WEIGHT OF THE EVIDENCE P 633, $2.84

"First-class puzzle, deftly solved. University background interesting and amusing."
—*Saturday Review of Literature*

Mary Kelly

THE SPOILT KILL P 565, $2.40

"Mary Kelly is a new Dorothy Sayers. . . . [An] exciting new novel."
—*Evening News*

Lange Lewis

THE BIRTHDAY MURDER P 518, $1.95

"Almost perfect in its playlike purity and delightful prose."
—Jacques Barzun and Wendell Hertig Taylor

Allan MacKinnon

HOUSE OF DARKNESS P 582, $2.84

"His best . . . a perfect compendium."
—Jacques Barzun & Wendell Hertig Taylor, *A Catalogue of Crime*

Arthur Maling

LUCKY DEVIL P 482, $1.95

"The plot unravels at a fast clip, the writing is breezy and Maling's approach is as fresh as today's stockmarket quotes."
—*Louisville Courier Journal*

RIPOFF P 483, $1.95

"A swiftly paced story of today's big business is larded with intrigue as a Ralph Nader-type investigates an insurance scandal and is soon on the run from a hired gun and his brother. . . . Engrossing and credible."
—*Booklist*

SCHROEDER'S GAME P 484, $1.95

"As the title indicates, this Schroeder is up to something, and the unravelling of his game is a diverting and sufficiently blood-soaked entertainment."
—*The New Yorker*

Austin Ripley

MINUTE MYSTERIES P 387, $2.50

More than one hundred of the world's shortest detective stories. Only one possible solution to each case!

Thomas Sterling

THE EVIL OF THE DAY P 529, $2.50

"Prose as witty and subtle as it is sharp and clear. . .characters unconventionally conceived and richly bodied forth . . . . In short, a novel to be treasured."
—Anthony Boucher, *The New York Times*

THE HANGING CAPTAIN P 548, $2.50

"This is a detective story for connoisseurs, for those who value clear thinking and good writing above mere ingenuity and easy thrills."

—*Times Literary Supplement*

Hillary Waugh

LAST SEEN WEARING . . . P 552, $2.40

"A brilliant tour de force." —Julian Symons

THE MISSING MAN P 553, $2.40

"The quiet detailed police work of Chief Fred C. Fellows, Stockford, Conn., is at its best in *The Missing Man* . . . one of the Chief's toughest cases and one of the best handled."

—Anthony Boucher, *The New York Times Book Review*

Henry Kitchell Webster

WHO IS THE NEXT? P 539, $2.25

"A double murder, private-plane piloting, a neat impersonation, and a delicate courtship are adroitly combined by a writer who knows how to use the language." —Jacques Barzun and Wendell Hertig Taylor

Anna Mary Wells

MURDERER'S CHOICE P 534, $2.50

"Good writing, ample action, and excellent character work."

—*Saturday Review of Literature*

A TALENT FOR MURDER P 535, $2.25

"The discovery of the villain is a decided shock." —*Books*

Edward Young

THE FIFTH PASSENGER P 544, $2.25

"Clever and adroit . . . excellent thriller . . ." —*Library Journal*

If you enjoyed this book you'll want to know about
THE PERENNIAL LIBRARY MYSTERY SERIES
Buy them at your local bookstore or use this coupon for ordering:

Qty	P number	Price
————	————	————
————	————	————
————	————	————
————	————	————
————	————	————
————	————	————
————	————	————
————	————	————
————	————	————
————	————	————
————	————	————
————	————	————
————	————	————

postage and handling charge $1.00
———— book(s) @ $0.25

TOTAL

Prices contained in this coupon are Harper & Row invoice prices only.
They are subject to change without notice, and in no way reflect the prices at
which these books may be sold by other suppliers.

**HARPER & ROW, Mail Order Dept. #PMS, 10 East 53rd St., New
York, N.Y. 10022.**
Please send me the books I have checked above. I am enclosing $————
which includes a postage and handling charge of $1.00 for the first book and
25¢ for each additional book. Send check or money order. No cash or
C.O.D.s please

Name————————————————————————

Address—————————————————————————

City———————————— State—————————— Zip——————
Please allow 4 weeks for delivery. USA only. This offer expires 1/31/85.
Please add applicable sales tax.